CONTROL ALT DELETE

CONTROL ALT DELETE
A GRAPHIC HALLOWEEN COMEDY HORROR

IVY GRAVES

ACKNOWLEDGMENT OF COUNTRY

The author acknowledges and pays her respects to the Traditional Owners of the land on which she lives and writes.

She extends her respect to all First Nations people and acknowledges Elders past and present.

For those who dwell in the darkest of shadows.

The Crows are watching.

So, slide into your mask and "Swallow, Kitten."

FOREWORD

Don't be T.R.A.S.H.

Transphobic, Racist, Ableist, Sexist, Homophobic.

LOVE IS LOVE

Save the Dolls and all of us who dwell between the
binary.

CONSENT MATTERS

Risk-Aware Consensual Kink (RACK) and Enlightened Consent are two current approaches for BDSM. However, the framework and language are always evolving. Please research your local legislation and peer reviewed articles on the subject.

Having capacity and ability, being explicit in communication, giving and getting permission. It is ongoing and retractable at any moment.

Safewords, the traffic light system, and other nonverbal signals are examples of communication.

YOUR FIRST WARNING

This is NOT a romance book. It is an extreme, graphic comedy about the underbelly of cyberspace.

I wrote this *dead lizard* for *whore-rawr* readers who have **zero triggers** — for those who don't need a happily ever after or even a happy for now. If you think you know what's coming, no you don't. If you have any kind of trigger, this book is not for you.

YOUR FINAL WARNING

Happy Halloween, my Little spooks and ghouls. **CONTROL ALT DELETE is aggressive body horror cloaked in dark humour wrapped in a Halloween mask**. From page one of this little woeful ditty, it will kick you in the nuts.

CONSENT MATTERS. ALWAYS. If you CONSENT to proceed and scare your eyeballs by reading CONTROL ALT DELETE, good luck getting to the last page without wanting to:

1) hurl chunks

2) punch Kitten in the face hole

3) jerk one out while having a panic attack

Congratulations, if you make it, you might just win a metaphorical gold star. Collect and cut it out at the back of the book.

Rated: 18+ Adults only. XXX. Graphic everything. This book should only be read in the stickiest of back rooms in dark alley smut cinemas ... somewhere in a Cyber Town far, **very** far away.

Giggedy.

THE CROWS ARE WATCHING

PROLOGUE

THE MURDER OF CROWS CLUB MEETING

THE SQUELCHING squish of testicles echoes around the stone room as I land my kick and giggle like a hyena. My foot aches as I step back on it, but the gathered voyeurs' combined laughter lets me know that I've hit my mark solidly.

I look around fondly at the room of women, all are high femme. Some with surgery, some without. Each observing from leather and velvet chairs scattered around my brand new dungeon, a small, fierce circle. Our web is cast wide.

We are here breaking in the facility.

Cracking some bubbles in celebration.

The scent of rubber, leather, and our perfumes mingles in the air as I scan their ecstatic faces for feedback. I wait breathlessly for my best girlfriends to rate my last stiletto blow.

We are justice seekers who speak the language of magic. We are the untamed wild feminine, watching from the shadows, shining as a mirror at inconvenient times. Our masks are many and varied, with one thing in common. We are all survivors.

Mistress Stitching says, "Ooh, I'll admit, that *was* a good one! That was a solid 9!"

Stitching's long brown curls fall over her bare shoulder; the other side of her skull is bald. She does it with a straight razor, and that's one of her favourite fetishes. Mine, too.

Looking down, I see yet another disposable man-child idiot, bound in my finest cotton candy ropes. The purest agony alight in his scarlet features.

"No way!" Says Paradox, her sadistic eyes aglow. Her tall presence is imposing. "That's a clean 10," she continues. "Look at the silly Tomcat, he still can't scream! He definitely needs to be neutered tonight. I'll help."

I clap my hands and bounce up and down and squeal, "Yes!"

Mistress Cane's commanding voice rises above us all.

"I'll agree, it was a great nut cracker, but definitely not a ten!" Every set of eyes swivels to watch Cane from her purple throne in the corner. Her posture rod straight, and her surgically enhanced lips a perfect shade of cool matte red.

Her long hair is braided and pinned atop her crown in an elegant swirl.

She says, "There's always room for improvement, Mistress. Never let your ego drive the show. Let's never get too cocky, or you might end up like this silly fellow."

She points at him as though he's nothing more than a speck of dirt. He whimpers softly as we all watch him.

"You're right, as always," says Goddess Paradox, gold jewellery jingling against her warm brown skin, as she gestures with her hands. "But the reaction she got out of his pathetic pink ass is worth five stars!"

We all nod, and the smile on Paradox's glowing face lets me know that everything is going to be okay. "Applaud for the five stars!"

They give me a golf clap and giggle.

"I'll take that. I'm not perfect, no one is, but I'm damn well very close!" I say, my hand on my hip.

My attention turns from my friends back to the bedraggled, wincing man, who is trying to keep his soul inside his body. He is grateful to be the focus of this entire spectacle, and I giggle at him as he continues to strain a smile through his exploding assault of pain. But he's desperate to please me.

He just copped the brunt force of my supple three-thousand-dollar boots, a combined gift from the girls.

"Thank you, Mistress," comes his pathetic groan.

I see my happiness reflected in his burning face.

"Did I say you may speak peasant?" I spit my words at him, then spit on him for real.

As it slides down his face, he doesn't wipe it away as he shoves his human snout to the floor. I glare at my rescued pet as an intimate circle of my girlfriends stands and gathers around me to watch him.

He's muttering, *"Sorry,"* repeatedly under his breath.

I boot him again in the ass, then ignore him and wink at my besties.

"Thanks for coming, everyone. I know some of you gave up work to be here. Your support means everything. This launch has been a long time coming."

They raise their glasses in a celebratory toast, and Cane clears her throat and looks directly at me.

"Congratulations, Mistress. I hope you enjoy these special gifts today. And I'm looking forward to our Smokers Lounge party coming up!"

"Me too, I'm cosplaying as a masked man!" I say, winking down at the man-child grovelling at my expensive feet. "It's all just a fucking game, isn't it?"

The women chuckle knowingly, as I stride toward the cowering man, my heels clacking off the cement.

I pretend I'm going to kick him, but pull up short. He's fun to scare. I hold my delicious boot up, exposing the sole toward him.

My voice is velvety as I say, "This is a fucking reward for you, Little Man. You have earned the right to lick now."

And the look in his sorry eyes tells me everything as they snap up to meet my own. He leans toward my outstretched heel, his pink tongue lovingly licking the dirt from underneath my shoe, and my pussy tingles as I watch his eyes roll back in his head.

I place my foot back on the ground, and he resumes his kneeling position, his cock now obviously erect and throbbing as painfully as his mashed nuts.

He understands how lucky he is, this rescue pet I have taken ownership of.

"I'm going to break you even more than you are now, you realise this, don't you? You're lucky to be here, amongst these strong and powerful women. Maybe you're not as diabolical as I thought you were when I started investigating you. Now, let's get on with this neutering. I have a special blade here, especially for this, your most personal of sacrifices."

His nuts shrivel into raisins as I laugh at myself, and my blood pumps a little faster as his panic attack sets in.

[1]

I SHRUG into my beat-up leather jacket and crunch on the strawberry and cream lollipop in my mouth. Once I hook up my Bluetooth in my helmet, I flick a couple of texts to the five chicks I've arranged to hook up with tonight. I snap a selfie with the bike, send it to them all, and pocket the phone.

The engine roars to life as I start it, and slide on my helmet, then gloves. I'm ready to get my dick slurped five times, and it nudges against my jeans. Throwing my leg across, I settle into the rumbling seat, and my Jacob's ladder vibrates with the thrum. It was so hot when that chick pierced my dick. Bit of a weirdo, but she was cool.

Mmm, I can't wait to fuck Callsign_GothPumpkinSpice or whoever she is, tonight. Her pussy is so pretty, I've seen all her dildo fucking vids. The ones she privately sent me, and was stupid enough to trust me to keep secret.

Yeah, fucken funny. This shit goes straight up on my dark website, and millions of creeps will be jerking off to her tonight.

I kick up the stand and take off into the night.

It's almost midnight, and most of them are already there. Waiting, with their plumped, glossy face and pussy lips, waiting for me to slide inside and thump all the way to pound town.

My firm thighs grip the bike, and the sensation almost makes me come. Zooming through the streets, everyone looks at me in awe as I fly past them. The John Wick playlist is belting in my helmet as the pink and green neon lights flash past, and before long, I arrive at the venue of the party.

I park down the road, because I don't want some shady cunt sniffing around my shit. I swap my helmet for the Jack Skellington mask on the back of the bike and head off along the road. I walk up the street, blowing grape smoke behind me, the way it smells reminds me of strip clubs and sex clubs. The goth bitches drip over this skeleton mask and these biker boots I'm dragging down the road.

I shove my hand in my pocket, running my fingertips across the tiny plastic bag that will make sure I get my knob slobbed at least five times tonight. A variety of multicoloured choices for my Little Whoever. Depends on her — or my — needs at the time.

I make my way up the dark path at the front of the house, music is blaring from the inside, and I jump as a giant skeleton lurches forward at me, shrieking, obviously on a motion sensor.

My heart shoots out my mouth as I continue up the driveway toward the party. I spot a couple of hot goth babes off to the side, eyeing me suspiciously. One is dressed as Poison Ivy, the other as Harley Quinn.

Huh.

I raise two fingers to my chin and stick my tongue out, pretending to lick their clits.

"Gigolo Warlock," they say in unison, then they both flip me the bird, cackle like witches, and then go back to talking and smoking.

"Dumb fucking bitches," I say.

What did I do?

Actually, one of them does look familiar. Might have fucked her somewhere along the way. Their laughter gets louder.

Those goth babes are hot in bed, though, little pixie freaks. I've licked plenty of their little rosebud pussies. They're into all kinds of creepy kinky shit, and my dick stiffens at the thought of tying them both up to that tree over there. Or chase them down the street, then fuck them in the gutter.

Sluts. They want me. They all do.

As I continue toward the music, there are a couple of circus freaks off to the side of the house, twirling hoops and fire on sticks. Dark throbbing techno vibrates through the ground as I get closer to the party.

I especially attract the dark romance bitches who are into somno.

I make sure my silicon mask is in place as I approach the average-looking inner west Sydney house. Cobwebs and spider decorations are everywhere, and floating ghouls and witches hang from the ceiling.

The base beats throb straight to my dick as I step through the front door and inside. It's dark, with black lighting making the skeleton costumes glow. All kinds of people pinch my ass, and my dick throbs. They think I'm so hot, so many masked babes dressed as slutty cats, witches, and serial killers with heels. None of them has any idea who I am, exactly like I prefer it.

I just told them all that I would find them; that's the thrilling part for them. They don't know who I am or what I've got planned. They said they read it in a book, and wouldn't that be fun to try?

They all sent me their pictures, so I know who I'm looking for, and my cock twitches at the thought. They said I can do whatever, throw them in the boot of my car, hogtied.

Dirty sluts. I'm here for every fucking one of them.

It's so much easier when they are into the masked man bull shit, I can get away with more. They want to climb me like a tree, and since I've got my new tats covering everything, they all turn around and watch as I pass them by. They can't help themselves; they want to fuck me.

My saliva flows when I think about the sexy peaches I'm going to stick my face in tonight, and I make my way through the crowd in search of these little kittens.

The girls' usernames flash in my mind like a list.

SubbyRope_kittensslut

Babygirl_Bunnybrat

ThickThighsNoEyes

Witchy_Brat_69

Callsign_GothPumpkinSpicemoonshine

Now, to find the first one. SubbyRope_kittensslut said she'll be dressed as a latex nurse. Now, I spot a girl wearing just that, standing in the corner. Drinking something out of a glass.

I run my fingers across the tiny plastic baggie again, and my cock swells again.

A dark plague doctor figure pushes past me and treads on my toe. A deep, mech robotic voice speaks from within the beaked leather mask, "Caution, game over is coming for you, bitch."

The temperature drops, as a sudden bout of nausea tries to escape. I swallow it down. That was close. The last thing I want is a bunch of puke swimming around inside my expensive moulded cosplay mask. These things cost a fortune.

"Hey, fuck off, dude. Watch where you're stepping," I say.

The figure turns and grips me by the forearm, leaning in close to my mask.

"No, baby," the freaky Plague Doctor voice says again. "You watch where you're stepping. Look down."

I look down to see three cockroaches climbing up my boot and onto my jeans. I shake my leg and look up, and the Plague Doctor is gone. The party music thumps around me, and I move on, girls and pussies and titties on my mind.

The next four hours pass by in a blur of drugs, booze, impromptu BDSM scenes, and fucking girls up against walls and trees. One even let me chase her down the street, then fuck her as I squeezed her neck in the gutter, just as I had thought about earlier.

It was so fucking hot. Awesome fucking night all up. The chicks were all dripping, and four of them were really great at blow jobs. My dick performed like the high-end porn star he is, and left a pile of women in one of the upstairs bedrooms, groaning in pleasure.

On my way out, I jog down the front path, but that Plague Doctor blocks my access.

"Fuck, here we go," I say to it.

"Hello, Kitten," the Plague Doctor says. "Have a nice party, did you, little manipulating anklebiter? Find your list of females?"

"Who the fuck are you?" I growl.

I look up at the mask, trying to see who it is. Wondering whether it's one of my gamer mates who recognises me in this Skellington mask.

"Did they get on their knees for you, Smoke Shadow Daddy?" the Plague Doctor says as they continue to block my path.

My vision spins. How do they know my handle?

"Did you get your dick sucked, babycakes? I watched your diabolical little show out on the street, by the way. It was hard to witness. But we're always watching you. Did you hear that girl saying no? What gives you the audacity? You're a fucking grenade, and you're dick's the pin. You'd best watch the way you treat women. Consider this your final warning from The Crows."

A cold shiver runs down my spine as the figure steps aside to let me pass.

"Pfft. Whatever, dude," I say, acting braver than I feel. I have no idea what they're talking about.

I want to throat punch this asshole, but a voice in my head warns me not to get involved. Maybe they're a fucking crackhead and will kidnap me.

I toss my empty beer bottle into a tree, glass shattering everywhere. Fuck them for scaring me.

I shake the creeps and stride down the dark drive toward the street. The stupid skeleton prop only adds to my fear as it jumps out at me, again.

That Plague Doctors' robotic voice calls from behind me. I don't turn to look.

"Karma is going to fuck you up, Smoke Shadow. The crows are watching, and we heard you're afraid of the dark! Uno reverse, bitch."

"Fuck off!" I shout, as I jog back to my bike, pretending to be unphased about that creepy asshole, but I'm rattled.

And what's all that crap about the crows watching me?

[2]

"Fucking bitch," I mumble the next night.

I tug my hood tighter and shove the door of the convenience store open, stepping into the cool mist. The multicoloured neon lights reflect on the wet streets, but my ears are warm under my headphones and hood, and I move in time with the techno beat.

I grab my skateboard from against the store's brick wall and kick off along the pavement. The wind whips past my face as the deck wobbles on its rusty trucks. I smoke and make a mental note to add a new board to my cyber wishlist. Some chick will get it for me, one of my groupies of the sinister dark web. Someone is always gonna give me what I want from now on. Maybe I should put some new shoes on the list.

A few of the sexy Spanish phrases I've been learning

15

from book chicks echo around in my mind. I was learning them earlier.

"Siéntate en los tobillos," I say.

Pretty sure that means get on your knees, bitch, or something. Actually, it was one of them that was teaching me how to say, "Get on your knees."

She was laughing the entire time she was teaching me and her friends were too. They all want to suck my cock. I'm so fucking sexy.

"Chupame la pinga bebe," I shout out loud as I whizz past houses filled with people sleeping. I can't remember exactly what that phrase means - suck my dick maybe? - but I'm sure it sounds right. Those baby girls won't know the difference anyway.

I slow down to round a corner, then kick off again to leave a trail of blueberry and mango smoke as I roll. Fuck, I'm hot.

I need to practise my Scottish accent later, to use on my fans too.

My dick nudges my pants.

I've watched a few videos by vocal coaches as well as a day or two on Duolingo. I'm a fast learner and only need to hear new words once. Also, my sluts are from different places around the world, so they teach me sexy phrases too.

As I grind and glide the last part of my journey through the cold streets, a white plastic bag of snacks is in one hand, and I shove the vape in my pocket. Kicking my skateboard up, I drag it over the front steps behind me.

Yeah, I could probably be in better condition than I currently am. I should quit the gardening and vape, but I'm fit. Fitter than the fat sugar daddies that get those sweet, sweet titties.

I'm what all the book girlies want. Tall, angular, hung, pierced, tatted. Plus, everyone says I'm gonna be the hottest narrator within the next two years, and I believe them. I'm that good.

The wooden apartment door slams, and I lock it, putting the keychain in my pocket. I have a bunch of E-girls stalking me at the moment, all part of the job, really. I slide my fingers across the cool steel chain. I wrap it around my fist like a rope.

My breath quickens.

I want to feel a chain wrapped around a pretty girl's throat. I want to watch as the air leaves her lungs for the last time. Eyes begging. Whatever, and I'll chase her through the moonlit woods, gagged and mascara running down her face if that's what she dreams about when she flicks the bean.

I'll rail her up the ass.

The chicks that stalk my livestreams every single night need every fucking inch of me.

"Mmmm," I hum, warming up my range for later, when I whisper vapid commands at the masses.

I kick off my shoes and pack a bowl, shove it in the bong and smoke it. Holding the weed in my lungs, I look around my pad, very happy with the foam covering every inch of my apartment. I've turned the entire thing into my own porn studio. I've got all the camera and audio gear. I'm exactly where I want to be.

I grab a cold can of OG Monster and crack it open. I slump back in my gaming chair and blow out a long stream of smoke, and slide my headphones on.

"Back," I say to the team. "Status?"

I take a sip, the sugar flooding my system and waking me up.

"Welcome back, loser," Callsign Rider says through the headset.

"Fuck off cockhead," I reply. "Who asked you?"

A snort, and I smoothly insert myself back into the game, as we carry on blasting the fuck out of a sprawling hoard of zombies.

"Did ya get any vids from that blonde you were talking to?" I ask Rider. "Fuck she had a nice set of titties. Hard smash, my bruh."

Laughter from the guys, and Callsign Miss Misery pipes up with, "Can you knobstains shut up about all the women you stalk? You're an idiot."

She's one of those weird little goth freaks, into all the same games as me. She's cool sometimes, but she's not really my vibe.

"Oooooooooh! You're not my real dad!" I say to her. "You can't tell me what to do!"

Miss Misery snorts. "Jesus fucking christ. You're a bunch of creeps. I have to remind myself we're not in a shit stained locker room, the way you carry on."

"Oh, Little Misery Guts, you're not passing the vibe check tonight. Suck my shiny metal balls. I'll shove my snake dick so far down your throat you'll be breathing out your eyeballs," I growl at her. "Fuck. I should come over there and teach you a fucking lesson, princess. I'm gonna tongue punch that little starfish till you scream for more."

I love shit stirring her.

More laughter from the dudes in the server.

"Fuck yourself," she says. I think I hear her sniffing, but can't be sure.

Is she crying?

We ignore her and carry on slaughtering the enemy and looting digital convenience stores.

"Ahh shit dude! I'm surrounded!" I scream. "Fucken things are crawling out of the drains! Rider, you there bruh?"

"Nah, man, I'm up in the car park."

"Fuck."

"I'm on your six fuckwad," Miss Misery says. "You're giving limp dick energy."

She comes blasting up from behind me and helps me shoot the brains out of the creeping zombies.

She tells me to go fuck myself a few more times as she saves my ass, before she mutes herself and goes AFK, leaving her character idle. I scoff and carry on playing without her, and my jaw hurts from laughing at all the dumb bitches we manage to offend without even trying.

That Misery gamer bitch is obviously jealous; she probably couldn't get laid even if she wanted to. She's never shown her face, which means she's gotta be some kind of ugly. So, I don't care about her opinion, anyway. Only the hot ones get my attention.

The sound of rapid fire fills my headphones, and I chat with Callsign Strawberry, one of the gamer girls I've fucked before, and definitely will again.

The multilayered screams fill my ears in sweet surround sound. I play for another hour, and I chew my way through half a bag of corn chips, before I begin to yawn. I call it a night when I notice the time and log off, making my way down the long corridor of my apartment.

My Late Night Spicy Masked Chat starts on all my platforms soon, and my cock hardens at the thought. My epic cult of feral ladies; each unique one ready to kneel and open their pretty legs and virgin holes for me. Each ready to fall in lust with me, then sit on my face in a week.

I pull the keychain from my hip again and jam it into the padlock next to the yellow sign that says FUCK OFF, RECORDING IN PROGRESS. I light up the red neon sign as I step in the door.

"Good girl," I say, clearing my throat and warming up my vocal chords. "You want this cock, don't you?"

Inside my spare room, a red lamp illuminates the corner in a warm glow, and a neat pipeline of white cable feeds into a power block. The long snake of extension cable disappears through a hole and inside my booth.

I scratch my new throat tat, and ponder how much cash I've sunk into this fucking Voice Actor setup, all my gym sessions, vocal coaching and the hours of tattoo sessions. My porn business has cost a metric fucktonne; a pain in the starfish to construct, but I got there, with the sexy details that matter to the females. And now it's starting to pay off.

I lower my voice and say, "Check, one two. Check, check."

I repeat this over and over, with different pitches and accents, and I vocalize as I glance around my studio. I see myself as a masked rockstar, standing on the stage at Wacken or some shit, bowing and jerking my cock at all the thousands of people who come to hear my awesome voice.

My dick jerks from a semi to a full-blown rager as I remember all the titties and tight pussies they have been sending me their selfies whenever I whisper *good girl*. I look at all my props and cosplay costumes, and the makeup area is off to the side, where I paint my eyeshadow and eyeliner.

All the mods I have, keeping an eye on my live streams, ready to open their holes for me, of course. They are the ones who taught me how to do my sexy masked-man makeup.

All those gorgeous women: all colours, shapes, hairstyles, languages. All of them have two things in common.

1) Their age — 21.

2) They're all submissive brats.

Just how I like them.

Yes, I've been busy. This sexy porn cult leader thing didn't happen overnight, no, no. This kind of shit comes from years of hard work, investing in my body, and behind-the-scenes dedication. Keeping spreadsheets and different apps to track all the women. All those times I'm trolling them, I have to make up new accounts, so I can approach them again, privately, and make sure I fuck around with my voice filters enough that they don't recognise me.

I've practised this charade and trained for this plan. I'm not dumb. I've pumped my iron religiously, and I get my cardio in.

Hey, I skated to the shop tonight instead of taking the bike. And I'm shredded, I've eaten more boring steamed salmon and fucking rice than I ever wanted to. But, it's not all bad. There are plenty of hotties in tiny little bras and shorts up their ass cracks that I can perve on the treadmill while I lift weights. Their cute jiggly thighs and tummies bouncing, and those pillow soft tatas bouncing too.

Mmmmm. Juicy thick bitches love to lick my ripped and tall physique. My fucking dick throbs painfully, and I rearrange it in my pants as I pour myself a shot of vodka and down it in one. I repeat the process and do a few vocal scales, practising my singing. I know I'm meant to avoid alcohol, only drink water and lemon, blah blah. But fuck that.

I can't wait to jerk myself off; my new dick tattoo makes me look even cooler. I cross the room to the booth and slide the door closed with an airtight swoosh. The scent of the pine frame and specialist audio equipment is mildly electrical and very expensive. I'm an expert in production now, but it's all been worth it.

Keep all the profits.

It's silent and dark here. I'm uncomfortable in confined spaces, especially if I can't stretch my legs out.

I can hear my heart thumping, and my rapid breathing slowly calms as I switch on the red lights, and pull on my skeleton mask. Reaching over my head, I remove my shirt, making sure my tattooed torso is in shot, and I slide my expensive headphones on.

This plan to keep my dick wet every single day of the year — if not once, then multiple times — has been brewing for years, and I don't rush things. I play the long game. I pace things methodically. I play these women off each other, get them to buy me expensive shit that I couldn't afford at my shitty office job in the city.

But, I gotta pay the rent, as well as all the new gear I'm having flown in from Europe. Can't get this specialist microphone shit from any old place in Australia.

Nah. It's complicated, and I figured it all out myself.

These dark romance readers are all hand-picked, little subbys, all of them lurking in masks and holding up signs to communicate. Ready to throw themselves at the feet of any anonymous profile with a deep voice or voice changer. Whatever. Chicks are dumb.

I found out about these dark romance girlies a few years ago, and something clicked. Especially when I realised that they all have a thing for dudes exactly my height, 6'4" or bigger mountain men. When they find out about my height, they swoon. It's fucken funny as... bruh.

They lean into my dominant vibes, my growly presence. Their tight tacos quiver, their panties are creamy every time I fuck their ear holes.

I swipe onto the app and click 'LIVE'. My image appears like a mirror, and I get the dopamine hit I need from my reflection. Red strip lights enhance the bad boy vibes, and I start up my playlist of sex tracks.

I pull the mic closer and turn up the reverb. I love how I sound when my levels are perfect.

[3]

MISS MISERY

I shove my wheely chair out from the desk, my blood boiling. Tossing the headset down, there is a red tinge to my vision covering everything, as I log out of the post-apocalyptic zombie game.

Callsign Smoke Shadow can go fuck himself up the ass with an aerosol can, or whatever it is he uses to keep his widdle-big-peeni rock hard.

Through tears, I glare at my old bald cat, who is sleeping in a cardboard box in the corner. My heart is heavy with grief, and a tempest is brewing.

I'm either going to dye my hair green, get a new tattoo, piercing, or rescue a new pet.

No. I'll drink some whiskey tea. That will help.

Heading into the kitchen, I rage clean the bench for a

while as I dissociate, listening to the kettle boiling and processing the emotions flooding through me.

As I spray and scrub my clean kitchen, my mind travels back to my ex. The way she preyed on me in the beginning. All the love bombing, all the right words and gestures and promises of everything that could make the world right. And then a few weeks after all that bullshit, that moment I walked in and found her. Crimson chunks dripping down the grubby white wall behind.

I turned and screamed into the night. Sobs from the past turn into tears of the present, and I hiccup and yawn as the flood of emotions passes. I wiped the plopped tears into the sudsy counter, allowing the unsolicited wave of grief to surge through.

That Smoke Shadow Daddy Twat is driving me insane with this gut-wrenching and heart-breaking limerence. I'm a fully grown, well-educated woman. Hell, I've almost finished my Master's in Nerdy Shit. Everything about Fake Dom Shadow Daddy is one walking red flag stitched together with the souls of the long lost matriarchy. He sucks the feminist right out of my left tit and slurps up the drops. 100% chauvinistic moron. So, why can't I stop stalking him in the fucking matrix? He thinks he's Neo, but he's fucking not. He's not the only one I watch, to be honest, I prefer watching women diddle themselves. Like one of my best fuck buddies. I think of her gorgeous tattoos, so gory, the way the artist made her joint doll stitches so realistic, so many shades of scarlet. A real life bride of Frankenstein, and I can't get enough of her. Women like her are what really get my juices flowing; they are where I should be laying my head at night.

So why am I fantasising about Callsign Shadow fucking me in the dark? I want him to hunt me like a fucking deer, like a bunny through the forest. Oh yes, with his fucking commando gear on, loaded up with weapons as he lassos me with his ropes, and pulls me in. The way he tears off my clothes as I scream into the canopies, the full moon above. I want him to shred me with his fucking giant Jacob's ladder.

I growl at myself and throw my hands in the air.

Men! My panties are damp, as I think about his cock again.

His Mummy issues are glaringly obvious in the way he interacts with the women in his space. I have a feeling that it's not just roleplay, I think he believes that a woman's place is at his feet and on her knees. The thought of his long dick makes my mouth water.

I sigh again, because I know he's just a sad loser in a hot body.

"This is bullshit," I say aloud to Fluff.

He raises his head to look at me, and then a noise from upstairs, but it sounds like one of the other pets. They're all locked in their separate cages at the moment, so I need not worry.

I blow my nose and wipe my eyes again, as I slide onto the burner phone in its red case. Red for giant walking red flags. I log into his late night platform and stare at him. This is the one I actually pay money for, to watch the special, subscriber-only, after-hours, jerk fest.

Well, he doesn't know it's Callsign Miss Misery. I change my name on this burner all the time.

I'm such a shit stirrer and pervert, but so is he and two can play this sordid game. I prop the phone up on the sparkling kitchen bench, which now stinks of fresh apple disinfectant; I make a pot of tea in my witchy teapot, and when it's brewed, I glug some Fireball whiskey into it.

Perfection.

Another glug of the hot spicy stuff, before switching off the lights downstairs and heading toward bed.

"Come on Fluffington," I sing-song to my eyeless, Sphinxish pet cat. "Time for bed now."

Fluffy Mcfloofenhousen Esquire the Sixth follows me up the red carpet stairs, meowing at my ankles to hurry up, herding me blindly to our boudoir. He's an old war horse, a real Tom cat, scratched up everywhere, but still has life in him. I rescued him as a senior, and he loves every fucking second he lives with me. I spoil my pets.

"I know, buddy, it's late. Sorry, I was torturing myself with Callsign Smoke Nincompoopy Face the Sixth."

I have to talk to Fluff so he knows where I am, poor old thing. He looks like a bald ballsack, and I hate him and feel sorry for him in equal measures. We met at the animal shelter after he'd been attacked by a pack of aggressive dogs and had his eyeballs removed. The group begged me to take him, saying a bullet was too good for him.

So here we are.

I juggle the teapot and my burner phone, settling into my cozy queen bed. Fluff curls up in his cat house, and I pour myself some tea and sit back. I grab my earbuds out of my bedside drawer.

I can't believe there are already 3000 people in his room watching, listening to him stroke his long sausage.

Makes me livid that idiots like him can earn so much money simply by lowering their standards with their voice and play-by-play commenting on their own masturbation.

The boozy tea warms me from the inside, as I snuggle into my blankets, and I slip my earbuds in. I giggle to myself about my little secret pleasure.

And now and then, on my trolling journeys, I come across an actual sexy one. Like this tosser.

My pussy tingles as soon as his dumb, husky, dusky voice enters my brain, and I feel my pussy drip, drip, drip.

Fucking Traitor. This is all your fault, Miss Pussy. Why do you always want to climb the tallest, prettiest jocks? Especially if they're a bully? Are my daddy issues that bad?

Yes.

I sigh, watching his subscriber-only, raging, feral, after-hours livestream. I've come to realise, he's got a few porn sets built into nice quality backdrops to go in his amateur porn videos.

Most nights, it's just him sitting in his black narration booth, sitting in his gamer chair jerking it, with his fake SWAT vest and ghost face mask hanging on the wall behind him. Or the lives where he's lazing in his gargantuan bed, like he is tonight.

I slug back some hot whiskey tea and settle deeper into my nest, studying his bed closely.

It looks sturdy, which is always good. There are obvious stocks in the end, solid wood, a hole big enough for a neck, and a smaller one on either side for the wrists. Would have cost a pretty penny, I can tell.

Why do I like to fantasize that I've got him bound in that bed, ass up in the air, as I ram into his tight little asshole with my giant pink strap-on?

He's shirtless, with a skeleton mask on the lower half of his face, pretty eyes peeking over the top, a fierce look of entitlement, and a huge helping of ego thrown in.

By the looks of it, the bed is more than big enough for my needs, cause I know he's 6'4" — he loves telling us all over and over how fucking tall he is. Like he loves telling his story about how he fucked his step sister last year. Or how he jerks himself off in the mirror.

He's so gross I want to scream, so why am I sitting here watching him all the time? Logging in to play games with him? Why do I seek his approval?

He doesn't care about anyone other than himself and his long dick. I can see off to the side of his bedframe are solidly fixed hooks, and lengths of chain coming off. With nice quality leather cuffs attached. I could put those to use.

At least he has some style. Something about him seems like he's not sitting in his mum's basement.

I have a feeling he has his own place. I've observed him interacting with women here, and I've seen some porn videos that he's posted that feature different women sucking his cock, kneeling next to him on that bed. I doubt a boy in his mother's basement would risk setting up that whole porn set.

"Oh, that's it, baby, you can take me. It will fit, just relax a little more, baby. Oh, that feels so good."

Ugh. He's so hot.

He sucks air in through his teeth, and I can hear the way he thrusts, the lube sliding up and down his long shaft. His goddamn Jacob's ladder reflects the red lights as his finger runs up and down.

I place the mug on the bedside table and lower my hand to my pussy, rubbing in small circles on my clit, dipping my fingers into my juices as I watch Shadow Daddy's huge cock thrusting up and down through his palm. The squelch of lube scratches an itch in my brain.

"Oh that's it, baby, just open that tight asshole a bit more, let me see those pretty tears streaming down your fucking face. Let me rub my fingers in there for you, oh, you love it, don't you babygirl?"

My rubbing gets faster, and my climax ramps through me without any effort at all.

Fuck.

As I relax back in my pillows, panting hard, I say, "I need to book myself in for some therapy tomorrow."

One of my other rescue pets, Noodle McTacopants, farts from his cage in the corner.

"Ugh, you're a gross guinea pig," I sneer.

He has luscious brown, white and black hair, which I like to run my fingers through, brush with a pretty pink comb, and put up in two pigtails for him. He's adorable.

His long brown beard reaches his chest, and I braid that for him, too. With a rainbow bow front and centre. He has his own viral social media accounts. People love the videos where I dress us up in matching clothes and sing funny songs.

I reach over and grab my fluffy slipper from the floor next to the bed, and throw it at his large cage. Metal rattles and he jumps and squeals a high-pitched, shrill sound, before hiding in the corner, terrified. Shaking in fear. As he should.

"Hey Noodle McStinkyface, know your place. You're lucky to be in my bedroom. You will be sent to the dog house outside with the really filthy animals tomorrow, if you don't keep that stench inside your body."

[4]

CALLSIGN SMOKE SHADOW DADDY

"Hey, my Little Shadows," I say, forcing the awesome fry in my voice, adding that sexy touch. "I'm you're Daddy. You are all beautiful and amazing. Thanks for being here. I will degrade you, you dirty fucking whore. Oh, you're such a good fucking bunny. Don't choke on it now. Goddamn. Oh, you wanna listen to me fuck your mind?"

Hundreds of users begin flooding into my room, as usual. Six hundred, eight hundred, two thousand. They're sending their thousands of coins and folding in half over my god given voice. This is why I don't have to work hard at my day job. I'll be able to quit that shit soon.

They're frothing at the mouth, gagging for me. I allow some of them up into my boxes, and I watch their wet lips open in awe, as they hide their burning faces behind their pointy manicured hands.

"Oh, you're taking it so well, baby, every fucking inch of me."

Their pussies dripping at my every word, dreaming of the night I'll come through with my promise of coming over to their houses and giving them a double hand necklace. Just like they read in their porn books.

"Welcome into the room PepperGirl666. Oh, Shygrrl_slut, thanks for joining us Little_MinxMouse204. Oh, thanks for the love hearts, Lexi_Toxicbabe. Thanks sweetheart, I appreciate you all more than you realise. Oh, now I need a big slurp of water. Do you have any idea what you're in for baby?"

My breathy laugh and practised vocals are crisp in this new mic.

I bring them all to climax with my voice alone, every night, I promise.

"Oh, you all just want to bend over for me, don't you Little Shadows? You want to feel me fill you up? I know you can take all of me, because you were made for me. Mmm, you BabyDoll_Tripper, you're so naughty. I'll spank you privately later."

Blood surges through me, and I grip my cock tight, pulling it out and squeezing. My voice drops an octave as I groan at the friction, pumping it a few times. I squirt some lube in my hand under the bench.

"Oh, welcome in my filthy little sinners. SMOKE SHADOW Daddy's home, who's gonna be a good girl for me tonight and get on your fucken knees? Open that pretty mouth for Daddy, right, fucking, now."

I am the hottest thing since dark romance was invented. And I'm gonna milk it for everything it's worth. Just like I milk my cock. They won't see me coming, and they won't see me leave.

"My little shadows, babygirls, babyboys and everything in between. And a special hello for my naughty little kitten. You know who you are. I hope you're drinking your water."

I rub my cock, veins pulsing — off camera, because the private show comes later, subscribers only — but they know what I'm doing under here. Jerking it. My hips thrust, they fucking love it, they're so wet for me.

"Oohh, that's it, baby. Right there, yeah, that's it. Just how I love it. Mmm, watch the dick piercings."

That's why they're all here, to picture themselves at the end of my dick, sucking, licking.

Watching me.

I stroke myself, rubbing circles on the tip, groaning unapologetically, and their lust and money flood through all four of my livestreams, as the women froth with fountains of hearts and devil emojis.

"Yeah, that's it, baby, spit on it," I say, as I spit into my hand and continue to rub my thick cock.

Pre-cum slips between my fingers, and I exhale as I picture the girls at home, flicking their clits.

ToxicGoldDustWoman sends me a private message, FUCK YOU'RE SO HOT, I'VE GOT MY VIBE OUT ;) and I read it on my second monitor as I watch the chat feed scrolling past. Lot's of females send me similar messages, and that thought makes me rigid.

Hell, I even think about all the guys, jerking themselves as they listen to my majestic voice order them around like the dirty whores they are.

"Now grab your rabbits and roses, and settle back into bed, my filthy little whores, and close your eyes. Listen to my voice as I talk you through this orgasm, baby. You want me to edge you? Don't you, fucking brats?"

I drop my voice till it's so low it's just a rumble they feel in their pulsating clits, "Oh, you're all my fucking Little Kitten's now, aren't you? So rub those wet fucking pussies for me and say, "Can I come yet, Daddy?"

My mods unmute all my little groupies at the same time, and I spurt my load onto my stomach, as dozens of girls' begging voices play into my shattering voice. Callsign_Bratty_Doll climaxes at the same time as I do, and the sounds of women orgasming fill my headphones. I pant, groaning for them.

"You're so fucking lucky to be here to witness this," I say.

I rub my jizz all over my six pack, before sliding two fingers in my mouth and sucking my cum into my mouth.

"Lucky fucking bitches. You better say Thank you, Daddy, for letting you watch my fucking show."

[5]

MISS MISERY

THE SCENT of petracor uplifts my mood, as I potter around in the drizzle and smile at my plants.

"Spill it bitch," I shout into my phone.

I listen to my friend chat about the previous night as I caress my plants in the back garden.

My succulent babies are happy in the greenhouse as I run my fingers across their juicy leaves.

"Wait a minute, I gotta pee." I place my phone and warm mug on the table and walk barefoot across the wet grass.

Connecting with the earth, I smile up at the grey sky.

I lift up my robe, and squat down, the cool air kissing my labia as I release a stream of urine, and I listen as it forms a puddle in the mud underneath me.

A fight between the dogs erupts in the kennel, probably a scuffle over a dry old bone. Usually, the alpha wins, but mostly he's so tired and sore he just ignores the younger mutts.

I stand up again, the last drops of piss dribble down my leg, and I lower my robe and skip back over the blossoming clover to my cup.

I love this house, these five quiet acres of rural property on the outskirts of Sydney, at the base of the Blue Mountains. It's been my dream for years to establish a rescue organisation that cares for senior pets, or those who are too aggressive to be out in polite society. I believe that there is good in everyone, even the diabolical amongst us. Everyone deserves a second chance, so I take in all types of animals. All shapes, sizes and breeds. I have enough space for everyone. Even those mongrels who seem to cause chaos everywhere they go, simply for existing.

I finish my morning coffee and head back inside, rinsing my mug out and wiping down the kitchen.

I finish the call and think ahead.

I have work today at the tattoo shop. I'm using their back room to do my extreme body mods. Today I've got a dude coming in to get some temporary piercings. He has an event to go to tonight, and he wants to feel good. I don't care why he wants the piercings, as long as I get to practise on him, and he pays me for the pleasure.

I'm sought after because not many people pierce cocks and balls and assholes. But I'll do anything. I don't give a fuck, especially if there is a room full of morally questionable men sitting next door, ready to help if some pervert decides to get a fucking boner when I'm piercing him.

I can look after myself, but I love the feeling of capable protectors.

Me and my damn bad boy obsession. And yet again, my mind spins back to Callsign Smoke Shadow Daddy cockface the second. Or third, I can't remember how many of them there are. There is one in every fucking game I scroll through or live I end up in the basement of.

Ugh.

My whisker biscuit tingles, and I chide her again. Fucking Miss Pussy, stop dripping down my leg. Stop dreaming about him sticking his face in you so you can ride his tongue like a damn riding bull.

If you let him fuck you, he'll do a destiny swap on you and leave you crying on the bathroom floor.

Keep scrolling. You're better than this. Don't get obsessed.

It will only lead to very, very dark places, for both of us.

But the place it will take him is far darker than he's ever dreamed of, sitting there in his fake SWAT vest and motorcycle helmet.

I doubt he can even ride a fucking bike. I'd win that fucking pissing competition. I haven't spent thousands of hours riding over the mountain pass for fun. I've outrun the cops more times than he can imagine.

[6]

CALLSIGN SMOKE SHADOW DADDY

THE NEXT MORNING, at my usual cafe, I wink at the new barista biatch as I collect my coffee from the counter. I slip her my card with my details and whisper, "It's best to get me on snap." I wink, and she beams, a blush rising up her neck and across her freckled cheeks, and her eyes dart around as she shoves my card in her green apron pocket. I don't look back at her, though I know she's still watching me as I make my way out onto the street and head towards work.

My Phonk_SlobMyKnob playlist blasts in my ears, and I trail vape smoke, backpack on. The coffee is burnt, and I wince against the bitter taste, disappointment flooding into my bloodstream instead of the caffeine hit I need.

"Just because a barista is hot doesn't mean she can make a good coffee," I mutter.

Into the office lifts and out onto level 24. I shut myself inside my cubicle box of doom and turn on my computer, and put my headset on. I want to be left alone today. Luckily, I'm in one of the back cubicles, where you can't see my screen, and because I'm smart, I'm up to date with everything.

Thank fuck for that, cause I don't plan on doing much actual work today. They don't pay me enough for that shit. I've got my own porn empire to build. On this international corporation's clock, mind you. I'm smart like that. I make everything fall into place. I've figured shit out. I'm a master fucking swindler.

These stupid middle management twats are as dumb as the baby brat chicks I fuck. They all think they're the boss of me, but I don't have a fucking boss and never will. One day, I'm going to be the CEO, and everyone can suck my cock.

And there are a few hotties that work down in HR, and a cute one in accounting too; she wears nice tight shirts.

I pull out my phone, swipe and check the messages on all my platforms. Keeping track of all the girls on rotation gets confusing and time-consuming sometimes. Not only remembering their online profile names and whatever hobbies they have, they all either like books, motorcycles, masks, or gaming.

As well as their profile names, I have to keep track of the 'special' cutesy names that I give them to make them feel special. I've studied the books, and I know all the pet names that make them feel unique, but I have to practise my lines.

So, I swipe open notes and check my NAMES list.

- Kitten
- Mouse
- Mamacita
- Pretty girl
- Little Owl
- Little Deer
- Little Doll.
- Pretty much anything with Little in front of it.
- Hell, I'll call dudes Little Man. I don't give a fuck
- Sweetheart
- Princess
- Bebe
- Sugar
- Dollface
- Sexy little ..... (add whatever word after this)

And then there are the ones who like baby, babygirl/babyboy/babyslut. Anything with Baby in front of it. But keeping names in order means my cock doesn't go a day without getting slurped, which is always my main goal. Cause the naughty little book lover's dream of slurping my cock, especially now that it's pierced.

And yeah, now and then their jealousy gets in the way of my dick-slurping extravaganzas, women's psycho bullshit when they think they 'own' me. They get in catfights over me. Who I love more? I tell them all I love them. It's bullshit, of course, but it gets my dick wet.

Bitchfights and catfights. But Callsign Smoke Shadow Daddy can't be owned. Not by anyone.

So when those annoying love attachments happen, and they get tired of the anonymous masked man sex, I drop those drags, block them on all platforms in case they dox me, and move the fuck on. I don't have time for that bullshit. I like things to keep moving in a big circle. In out.

Always a rotation of bratty little hotties to choose from.

My phone dings and I swipe the screen, thinking it's going to be one of the sexy little bitches I hooked up with this past weekend.

A message from Pepper_GOODGIRL. I call her my Little Kitten, and she blushes when I do.

> Hey Shadow Daddy. I'm
> available this weekend.
> Hbu?

Yes! I've been wanting to taste this stunning cutie for a few months now. She's been a bit cagey, but wearing her down with my manipulation skills has worked a treat; she's whispered her darkest thoughts to me.

Bingo!

She said she's been hurt by men in the past, yadayada. I can't remember the details; they all merge into one, but I know she uses a walking cane most of the time. She thinks that will be a problem for me, but it's not, not at all. I can handle anything that comes my way.

I shoot back a message to her, my dick nudging against my pants as a new selfie of her pink nipples pops up. I snap a fresh shot of my dick and send it straight away. She loves that shit.

> How about Saturday? Where u
> wanna meet?

Yours?

> Oh, ok then. Let's do this.
> How's 8pm ?

Perfect. See you then, sexy
Shadow Daddy. I'll wear
something cute ;)

> Oh, looking forward to it,
> Little Kitten.

Meow Smoke Shadow Daddy. My
pussy is waiting for you.

I shoot her my address, a new selfie of my dick, and extra details about how to find the right intercom button for my apartment when she gets here on the weekend.

Next, I doomscroll through all the titty and pussy shots she's sent me privately over the last few months. I should be working, but I can't be bothered. My nuts tighten, and cock throbs at the thought of tasting that sweet, sweet pussy.

Gently, I place my phone on the desk. I lean back and exhale. Shit, it's almost too easy.

Some other rando chick is heading over tonight. She's a little redheaded sweetie, aged 21, which is totally my type. She loves being spanked over my knee while I finger her tight little holes, and she squeezes around me as I fuck her nice and slow.

Work passes quickly, and I make my way home to get ready for my visit tonight.

I've fucked this little cutie before, don't actually know her real name, don't give a fucking shit. I call her my juicy Little Berry, and she seems to eat that up, like she eats my dick. As she should.

I met her online a few weeks back, and she has some of the sweetest suction between those juicy, glossy pink lips, and my cock throbs again.

I let myself into my apartment, toss my bag on the floor, and head straight to the shower. I've been so horny lately, watching myself back on video, listening to my sexy voice, and I slide into a recent vid of me jerking one out and prop my phone up so I can watch myself through the foggy shower glass.

My throaty grunts and groans reverberate off the tiles, soaping myself up and jerking one out exactly at the same time I shoot my load in the playback.

My stomach growls, so I throw down an egg and a bowl of ramen, brush my teeth and spritz in some spearmint gob freshener.

The intercom buzzes, and I check the security screen before letting her up. I put on my skeleton mask, and a knock at the door.

I let her in, telling her to get on her knees, right there in the entrance to my apartment. She loves every second of it as she slurps my knob back, right there on the hard concrete floor.

I bend her over the furniture before tying her up in my huge bed. I even cuff her, spreading her legs, before plowing into her. I don't really care that she squeals, and I don't use safe words. They're for pussies.

As I fuck her, I whisper sinister scripts I've written, about how I'm going to chase her through a haunted house at midnight. Pretty sure she was into it.

I tell her to leave. She pouts, like I'm going to ask her to fucking marry me or some shit.

I don't care how she gets home. I threw her out barefoot, with her heels in her hand. She's technically an idiot, I mean, an adult, so she's in charge of her own life. Her dad or brothers should be keeping tabs on her. She's not my wife. Not my circus, not my fucking problem or whatever that saying is. I should look that up.

My dick has been milked and exhausted, I crash back into bed, lying my head on my black silk pillows, and into a horny sleep. A montage of voluptuous beauties rotates through my dream, all naked, wearing sparkly pink high heels. A big lineup of them, like I'm the fucking king or president or rockstar or some bullshit.

No, I'm a fucking military dude, all sexy running with my guns hanging off me just like in my game. Yeah, I'm in my game dream, I'm walking between this aisle of naked bitches, all different colours and shapes and languages, and they all want me because of my hot, shredded abs, and my sexy V that they all fucking love for some reason, all these chicks on their knees, juicy mouths wide open.

I get to choose which one I want. I walk along, making my choice like I'm in the fucking chocolate factory. My dreams have come true, my hours of construction with the acoustic foam paid off, and it's all because I can lower my voice, even if my sexy fry shreds my vocal chords to shit.

This dream is awesome, I love lucid dreaming. I think it might be a wet dream if it keeps feeling this good. As I walk through this endless selection of chicks, I just growl, 'Babygirl' over and over in different pitches and accents, or 'Little Kitten,' they are all dripping pussy juice down their naked thighs, oh those sweet virgin holes are all lubed, wet and ready for me to just slide right into.

Oh yes, I'm the fucking king of voice acting and porn. No one is hotter than me, especially no one can compete with my unique fry.

[7]

MISS MISERY

I MAKE a couple of unboxing videos for my grotesque prosthetic makeup channel, and edit some more content for my new taxidermy vulture culture channel. Everyone loves my weird ass bone jewellery; they can't get enough of my leather cuffs and collars, especially the ones with the bones.

After I upload them, I feed the pets and clean out their cages.

I'm meeting the girls for a drink, and smoke and a debrief tomorrow morning.

A few ridiculous dick pics turn up in our group chat, and everyone laughs and sends funny memes back and forth.

I pack my separate body mod kit, filled with all kinds of needles, scalpels, alcohol wipes and other paraphernalia that cost me a lot of money to set up.

But now I'm exactly where I want to be. I have learned and practised the skills I need to achieve my goals.

I smile as I pour myself a mug of tea and wrap my hands around the mug. I sniff the spices and dissociate as my mind wanders with plans for the future.

There are a few more pets I'd like to welcome to the family. Adopt into the hoard of strays I've managed to accumulate over the last few years.

I drink my tea and swipe into some NSFW chat rooms, keeping tabs on the creeps and perverts.

Messages on all the platforms. Whispers and chatter about what it all means.

The Crows are Watching.

[8]

I FLICK a few more DM's to some indie authors to see if I can read their books on live, and slide into some new cute young female voice-over artists and see if they'll send me some tittie pics, or see if they want to slide onto Discord and have a private video chat with their vibrator. They all froth over my gravelly voice.

Realising the time, I jump up to smooth my black satin sheets. She'll be here soon. My dick pulses at the thought of the upcoming blowie. I whisper to myself, practising various French phrases that make the girls cream.

The sharp buzz on the intercom lets me know she's arrived, right as I'm lighting a sexy pumpkin spice candle. The chicks love the holiday candles, that much I know. I cross the room, buttoning up my shirt, leaving most of them open. Bad girls love my tats.

Pressing the button on the intercom, I snarl into the microphone, dropping my voice. "You're ten minutes early, aren't you, my good Little Kitten?" I make my voice really breathy, so she knows I'm erect and ready to fuck.

A giggle from the vixen in the monitor downstairs, I see the top of her blonde head on the black and white surveillance monitor, and my cock stiffens even more in my boxers. Mmm, I'm looking forward to this blowjob. I wonder if she's into wasabi. Shibari. Whatever that rope shit's called.

"It's Pepper," comes the sweet reply on the intercom speaker.

Yep, that's her!

"Come up!" I say in my sexy voice.

I buzz the front door and spin around, checking myself out in the mirror. I flex my muscles as I roll my shirt sleeves up to my elbows and place my brand new gas mask over my face. It's an awesome aesthetic I've got going on tonight.

A few minutes pass before a gentle knock at my apartment door, and I look through the peephole to see nothing. I frown, then her finger pulls away to reveal her gorgeous, long blonde hair. My view through the hole is blurry, but it's definitely the same chick that I've been video chatting with for a while now.

I unlock the door and pull it toward me, opening it wide, and I see my Little Peppery Kitten leaning back on a walking cane, the bottom of a black stiletto heel held up in the air. My mind freezes, and I do not compute. The hairs on my arms stand on end, and my sphincter puckers, before pain stings through my ribs.

I'm winded as I'm thrown backwards onto my ass, and I roll to crack my skull against the floor. Lights flash in my head, gasping to breathe. I struggle against shooting pains. My chest is on fire.

Before I can comprehend what's happening, a zap and a forceful jolt scorches my body as she tasers me, laughing as she does so, and I feel piss warming my jeans. I shake and stiffen, watching as she laughs, every muscle contracting, then nothing.

My head throbs, and I open my eyes to see my gas mask on the floor next to my head. Then I see giant thigh-high boots, laced up the front, and a sparkly walking cane covered in tiny diamonds. I get a flash up her skirt, her thighs are well-defined muscle.

She's hot, but the cane catches my eye again. It's swinging around and around in a blur, just like a cheerleader's baton as she shuffles a little tap dance in front of me. How long was I out? I see my keychain dangling around her neck.

I struggle with both arms tied behind my back, something hard pinching my wrists, and my feet tied with plastic zip ties.

"What the fuck, lady — " I grunt, mouth drier than a nun's cunt, before a cough racks its way violently through my fried body. I gasp for air, but it feels like there is no oxygen in the room.

The bitch is standing there wearing one of my own masks, the one I was wearing just last night. The skeleton one that all the gamer girls love.

"Hey, Pepper Kitten! That's my favourite mask, don't get it dirty! Who are you anyway?" A stab in my ribs as she kicks me again. I groan, rolling around, tears leaking out. "Why are you doing this to me?"

"Catfish!" She sings. "Gotcha, babycakes."

I've got nothing to say to that as she stalks around the room, laughing and snorting at me. She's enjoying this so much she needs to stop and bend over, leaning on her cane to catch her breath. She takes out a phone and snaps a picture of me, tears and blood on my face.

"Who are you?" I repeat, angry that she won't answer me. But again, she ignores the question as she wheezes and pulls an inhaler out of her pocket. I watch as she shakes it, inhales, and slips it away.

"I'm your karmic backfire," she says. "Your survivors are interested in updates about you."

"What's that mean?" I ask.

She carries on. "Thought I'd be a nice little kinky submissive brat, did you? Thought I'd get on my knees for Shadow Daddy, wet for your deep voice? Thought I'm popping round to perch myself on your throbbing pink dick? Make you feel like a real bad man? You're nothing but a bully, preying on the weak and traumatised, and I'm here to knock you down a few pegs."

She's mocking me. I can't believe it.

She starts singing, "Here comes the sun….dooo dooo dooodooo."

I cough, then say, "Oh, for fucks sake. I don't get it. You were so into me for the last few months, all those times we video called in the dark, when I jerked myself for you, and talked you through multiple orgasms. You love my voice, I heard you loving every second of it."

Her laughter ramps up now, fear creeping over me. Another well aimed stiletto kick to my ass. Oh shit, I've fucked up. Big time. This isn't the first time she's done this to someone. Not like all the pathetic other chicks I've fucked over the last few years.

"Oh, honey," she says, in a voice I've never heard her use before. It's lower than usual and unnerving. "Voice acting is just one of my many, many talents. You think you're the best narrator out there? Well, allow me to introduce myself, motherfucker. I've had over twenty years in the sex game. Many years on the phones and cams. I've done heavy scenes in the best dungeons worldwide."

She stops to lean on her cane and catch her breath, and I'm smart enough not to make a single peep. I realise I'm even holding my breath to see what she's gonna say next.

She smiles and continues speaking, more quietly this time. I can barely hear her, but I'm terrified. "I've flogged the sweaty balls of the country's top lawyers and judges; they all handed me envelopes stuffed with more cash than you earn in a year at your little job in the city. I've dressed those lawyers and judges — stripped them out of business suits and helped them into pink frilly dresses — and skipped them around town at noon. They all worship me. Pay ME to kick them, so listen to me, real good princess. This isn't my first rodeo, oh sorry, what was your stupid name for me? Little Kitten? Little fucking Kitten my ass. You're so full of yourself. Well, I won't charge you for this extended session; it's my treat. I created it just for you, and named it my *Fuckaround and find out special!*"

She looks around at the grey acoustic foam that makes up my apartment walls. Yes, I made it for my narration, but it's great to stop the neighbours calling the cops every time I bring a chick back here to fuck. Cause I make them scream when we fuck.

"Nice soundproofing," she says wryly, pulling the skeleton mask up over her head, and I notice the crow's feet lines around her eyes. I grind my teeth. She nods, a scary smile on her twisted face.

"You're not twenty-one!" I shout at her, my chest filled with pure burning hatred. "Your profile said you were twenty-one, you can't do that."

She ignores me. "That sound-dampening foam is going to come in handy for me over the next few days—"

"Few days? What the fuck did you just say?" I growl at her, that usually works.

Her glossy candy-pink lips form a crooked smile, as she reaches into her bra, she produces some black pills, the size of horse tablets, holding them between her long nails. "Oh, I've got lots of plans for you, my little shadowbaby." She lunges at me, her eyes dark and terrifying, and I try to shove her off, pushing back at her with my weight, but she grabs my jaw and squeezes, kneeling on me.

Oh my god, this bitch has got a man's grip on my jaw. Who is she? I grunt and groan at her, but the burn of her grip has me squealing like a little pig. I hope she never holds my testicles in that vice-like grip. She forces the bitter pills into my mouth, holding my nostrils closed, my tongue lurching forward spit them out, but she sharply grips my lips shut tight. With her other hand and says in a terrifying voice, "Swallow, Kitten."

What the fuck are they? Poison? Her long, pointy fingernails stab into my chin, and I scream out in pain as I realise she's pierced my flesh. She's wearing some leather fingerless gloves, each with some kind of metal thing protruding. Now I get how she punctured me. She's fucking batshit.

She leans over an inch from my face, her eyes showing just a glimpse into some kind of heavy background, and suddenly I need to shit. She snarls and then spits in my face.

She's like some jacked-up Sarah Connor combat chick, smooth, capable, and streamlined in every action.

My scalp is on fire as she tears my head back, and I cough, gagging as the pills choke their way down my neck.

She licks the blood dripping in rivers down my chin, then shoves me hard, releasing me, allowing me to gulp in oxygen.

She says, "You feel like you can bully people. Do whatever it takes to get your dick sucked. With your deep sexy voice, you think it's going to work on me?" She snorts. "You're a pathetic little weasel. You don't even deserve to lick the dirt off the bottom of my boots. That would be a privilege for you."

"You're a fucking pig!" I scream, sweat dripping, and pain searing in my chest. My muscles ache. She laughs at me.

"I think that's Queen Pig to you. Put some respect on my name. You're a tyrant, but that ends with me."

She twirls her glittery walking stick, laughing. She lunges back, and the sparkly cane comes for me.

[9]

BACK AT MY beautiful house in Kirrabilly, I recline in my green velvet wingback chair, looking across the harbour to the Sydney skyline.

Reaching across to the antique side table, I grab a small bunch of firm green grapes, and a small slice of brie on a cracker.

One of my naughty domestic submissives Jamoa bathes my tootsies in a rose scented bath. His cheeky grin spreads across his brown face, and I catch the glee in his amber eyes.

Strong, thick fingers massage my tender arches. I sip my gin martini. Stirred not shaken — so basically just a mouthful of booze. I swallow and sigh blissfully as the virile man's thumbs work their magic up my calves, releasing the tension.

I've already taken my pain meds for the day, and the little fun I had earlier at the dumb Smoke Shadow's house has taken the last of my spoons. So this luxury is divine.

"You've been good pupcakes today. I'm proud of you both. I might even let you rail me in a sundress one of these days, Hemschris."

I wink as his hungry gaze meets my own, and his shaggy hair falls across his face like sand dune ripples. He strides back and forth in the kitchen, preparing all kinds of things. I watch like a starving cougar, inhaling all six feet something of his spectacular naked form, naked but for his cock hidden behind a frilly apron.

"Thank you!" he says.

These men are walking around in the skin of Adonis, with a cock the length of a firehose. Hemschris is always wanting to dress in full black combat gear, boots, pocket pants and harnesses loaded up with an array of firearms.

I like teasing him occasionally, putting him in matching bralettes with Jamoa, and dressing them up like twins.

I'm a sick fuck. No doubt because I'm capable, strong, and too smart for my own fucking good.

But not now; my boys are looking after their Goddess, and in return, I'll take care of their primal desires. I look after my pets, yes, I do.

"And you," I say to Jamoa between my feet. "You've been a good boy too, you might deserve to lick my pussy."

He bounces up and down on his knees, unable to contain his pleasure. He's my Malinois, fierce, loyal, and competent.

"You're a sweet pup," I tell him. "A very *very* good boy indeed."

I lean forward to scratch him under his chin, and he riffs some nonsense monologue in various voices and accents.

"I am a good boy, aren't I, Goddess? I'm the best." He glares across at Hemschris, who just rolls his eyes, before looking back at me and continuing. "I definitely deserve to lick between your holy thighs. I kneel here, bowing before you. My Fierce Queen and God. I am devoted only to you."

He pulls back, drawing my rose scented, wet foot up to his mouth. I lean back against my oversized axolotl squishy, which makes me feel warm and fuzzy. Safe.

That's why these boys are here, adoring me in my private quarters.

He kisses each toe lightly, and I giggle, then say, "One little piggy, two little piggy." He smiles and his tongue emerges; he takes my big toe into his mouth, and I feel his tongue swirl seductively, warm and delightful.

Holding eye contact with me the entire time, he then starts to suck, and I begin an orgasm deep inside me.

His hefty cock throbs desperately inside its pink silicone cage, and I groan gently, knowing exactly how much this arouses all of us. "Good boy," I groan. "Keep sucking until I say you can stop."

"Hemschris, bring that rigid cock over here and put it to use, Jamoa's ass is feeling a little lonely, isn't it babycakes?"

Jamoa pouts and nods his shaggy head. "You need your asshole filled by Hemschris tonight?"

He nods, my toe bobbing up and down in his mouth, as Hemschris unscrews a jar of coconut oil and smears it all over his now fully engorged cock.

He smiles his Hollywood grin and aims his sword straight at Jamoa's hunched form.

I giggle to myself sadistically as I ready myself to watch this live porno.

[10]

SITTING IN MY GAMING ROOM, pink kitten ear headphones firmly over my ears, I wander around my Animal Crossing house, tending to the serial killer living in the basement, and squash the cockroaches that are running over the floor.

Squish squish squish.

Fluff is asleep in a ball in the corner of the room, and I sip my rum and coke and light up a joint.

My friends are all complaining about mean-girl bullshit going on behind the scenes of the book community. Picking sides against bullshit. It's cracking down the centre — a civil war, wedges driven between powerful communities. Evil infiltrates from within, like a rotten apple in one barrel. All of a sudden, everyone is inhaling weird parasitic spores.

"I'm just in hermit mode," I say to my friend on the headset.

"Same, fuck everyone. Trust no one. Keep hope that good people exist. I've found you haven't I? You have been consistently both a shit head and my best friend."

"Bitch, same."

I water my strawberry patch again and smile. I ash the joint in my green alien ashtray.

Come and get me aliens. I'm ready to leave this burning rock.

[11]

KITTEN SORE TUMMY THE FIRST

As my eyes crack open this time, it takes a while to adjust. Something heavy binds all four of my limbs. I tug my arms and legs again uselessly; I'm chained to my sexy BDSM bed. With my own lambswool, leather cuff restraints, and the fixings I drilled in myself.

"Fuck," I say, peering into the darkness. I scan for the Scary Pepper Cane wielding woman, listening for any tiny sound that will let me know what the fuck is happening to me.

The whir of my tower computer fans and various quiet beeps from messages are all I can hear. My gaming keyboard is flickering its waves of red lights, and I groan.

"Hello?" I say, struggling with the chains, unable to believe a tiny woman out foxed me.

Trying to sit up, I fail miserably. I'm so thirsty. How long have I been here?

I'm spread eagle with a cracking migraine, and secured tightly. I need some painkillers and a bong or four. I can even see my bong in the corner, and I can't even get there.

And now is when the panic really sets in, my breathing ramps up and sweat pours over me.

I try to focus on my computer keyboard, but it all swirls like a bad trip or sleep demon nightmare. I'm not going anywhere.

"I can't breathe," I gasp. I need help.

How long have I been asleep? How am I getting out of here? When is she coming back?

Shit, what were those drugs? There is something hard on my cock. I wriggle my hips side to side, it flops heavily, and with a looming dread in my gut I realise there is a metal cage trapping me inside. Oh no, what the actual fuck?

"Help! Anyone!" I scream out, wondering if that chick is still here. Are my balls going to drop off? I hear my computer continue its beeps and dings with messages from my friends on various platforms. All wondering where I am. It's dark so my followers will be waiting for me, pussies wet. I should be online by now, making cash. Getting ready to fuck another rando pussy. And now I'm hostage in a soundproofed hell of my own, well built, construction.

"Heeelp!" I scream again, but I know no one is coming to save me. Because no one can hear me. Let's face it, I've pissed so many people off over the years, no one would come anyway. Even if they could hear me.

A voice crackles through my surround sound stereo. It's her, Pepper Bitch.

"Hi, Little Kitten, have you been a good baby for your pretty Mummy?"

I strain to look all around, twisting my body as best I can, but no one is here.

"Where are you?" I yell. I can see the little red light of my gaming computer lit up, plus a few other red lights around my room that I know I didn't put there.

She can see me and she's talking to me.

"Where are you?" I scream. My gut churns, what is going on?

Nothing. Silence. The computer whirs. I begin to wonder whether I just hallucinated that whole thing, but then I hear my own voice, playing loudly over my speakers.

"Where are you? Where are you? Where are you?"

My own voice sounds desperate, scared.

Over and over again she plays my pathetic, choked sobs.

Chills run down my spine. What has she done? My voice

rings out again, but this time it's a voice clip from a few minutes earlier.

"Help! Anyone! Help! Anyone! Help! Anyone!"

God, I sound pathetic.

She shouts again somehow through my speakers, "What do you want from meeeee?" She's howling with laughter, then it sounds like she's wheezing, then she adds, "Aww, thanks Kitten, I've always wanted to try that line out on someone. You've given me a laugh. Good boy."

More laughter, and I'm about to shit myself because my guts are warning me that this lady is completely loco.

I hold my breath, trying not to whimper. Somehow, I don't think my sexy Spanish phrases will get me far with this one.

Some old audio clips begin playing loudly on the stereo now, and I cringe as I listen to the stupid shit I've said over the years.

"Oh, you won't need a safe word with me, whore. I'll fuck you into the fucking ground."

She keeps playing my dumb rantings on repeat for a while, and I can't do anything to stop it. Finally, it goes quiet again.

"Oh, who hurt you babygirl?" she carries on. "You're gonna be okay. Mommy's here, watching over you every minute of the day and night, and I won't let anything happen to you, until the time is right."

I feel piss trickling down my thighs again. I didn't even realise I'd done it. I hear myself sobbing like a fucking loser.

"Oh no, did the little kitten dribble from the cage? I'll have to remember to bring the plug next time. You're into sounding aren't you? I'll bring my violet wand kit when I come back, so we can jazz you up a bit. And I'll make sure to update all your loyal fans of your current predicament. Don't worry, I'll be doing a takeover of all your social media accounts, one of my friends is onto that for me as we speak. I'm setting up a sleep cam so we can all monitor you 24/7. You love people watching you jerk it don't you? I know, it's not your usual marketing angle, with your flak jacket and fake weapons, but who knows? Your little sluts might like to strap on, and fuck SMOKE SHADOW Daddy up his tight little virgin ass."

I cringe and attempt to call her bluff, "You wouldn't touch my ass!"

But something deep inside tells me that this Pepper woman does not fuck around.

"Oh, your eyes are gonna look so fucken pretty when they roll back for me, babygirl," she says. "I'm gonna rub your little prostate till you're spurting everywhere."

I scoff, but her seductive voice pulsates violently through my cock, pumping blood and desire, and angering me at the same time. Damn her and her awesome voice acting skills.

Her laughter tinkles through the speakers, and merges with the sound of *'Respect by Aretha Franklin'* begins playing around the room, louder than I play my own music, and that's all I can hear now as the song plays all the way through, and then starts up again on repeat.

[12]

MISTRESS CANE

I LEAN my plump ass against the kitchen counter as Jamoa finishes clearing my breakfast dishes. He's one of my favourite eye candies, and having him around my house is purely selfish. I love watching throbbing young men swanning about my space.

He's one of the many men that I keep on rotation. Any of them would drop everything to please me.

"Jamoa, my dear. Would you mind popping to the pet store and picking up some cat items for my new foster cat?"

"Yes, Goddess," he says, smiling knowingly as he wipes the bench. "Looking forward to this one."

"And Hemschris, here's a list for you." I pass my other house-slut a piece of notepaper with a list. "Would you please pop into the adult store for me, take my card. A bunch of cat plugs and a new pink kitten tag with

RESCUE CASE OF MISTRESS CANE engraved on it. After that, feel free to have the afternoon off. I have somewhere to be after eight. And you're both coming with me to help."

Hemschris says, "Oh, I'm looking forward to this too. Can't wait to see the new Kitten's face."

My good guard pupcakes go about their chores, as I have a lazy morning in my pyjamas.

One of my clients is taking me out for a fancy lunch and Jazz Club trip at a new speakeasy that's popped up. But before that, he wants to dine me at a silver service place, feed me lobster, and tell me how beautiful I am.

Who am I to decline such an invitation?

[13]

MISS MISERY

SITTING IN MY GARDEN, the wind blows my hair across my face, and the broken palings of the old fence rattle loudly.

I pull my hand-knit shawl around my shoulders a little tighter, and hum an old twisted nursery rhyme, as I poke around in my memory, trying to remember every last detail of last night's fucked up dream.

I scribble in splotchy ink in my Nightmare journal.

MISERY'S BOOK OF DEATH AND NIGHTMARES

She was all cupcakes and lollipops, spicy chilli and frothy bubbles of champagne.
And then everything turned to shit.

The grungy walls covered in guts and yoghurt and art.

Running through midnight dystopian streets holding a dead human body in my hand. It's the size of a skinned rat, oozing blood and vitriol. It looks like Rhiandra. My fingers sink into her guts, into her bleeding warmth, and I feel it throbbing in my palm.

I can taste her.

That gamey taste of heart.

That rich pop of the delicate muscle as I chew.

Torrents from my hand, leaving a trail where I run.

And something is tracking me with military-grade precision. A man. A hunter. A devious narcissist who sees right through me.

I need to take care of this beating sack in my hand, my lover, my ex girlfriend.

I can save her, bring her back from the dead.

So I put her in my apron pocket

where she can be safe. A tiny human body; someone I loved once, the shape of an anatomical heart.

Pumping.

Pulsing against my skin.

I'm the monster; the hideous beast people run from.

I'd fry her up for breakfast, served with eggs and beans, and freshly squeezed orange juice warm from the tree in my yard. I'd add ice cubes. Grilled tomatoes and a side of mushrooms. And my sweet Rhiandra's thigh sizzled just right in the pan.

Oh yes, my little ratty lover, I'm frying you up and having you for a late breakfast for supper.

[14]

MISTRESS CANE

IT's busy tonight at the warehouse, as usual all the different play rooms are fully booked with a full crew of security dotted about the premises. I spritz perfume across my chest, and blot my matte red lips with a tissue.

"He's ready," Mistress Dahlia says, popping her brunette head around the door. "Told him to shower and get in position for you in the holding cell room." Dahlia has been apprenticing under me for four years now, and she's just getting ready to spread her wings and fly without old Momma Cane. I've been contemplating a gift to give her, when she's ready to go out on her own.

"Thank you Dahlia. I'll leave him squirming as he waits a few more moments for me," I say, raising my martini glass at her in thanks. "Make him even more terrified about what I may have planned."

She laughs and double taps the door frame, before disappearing down the corridor and back toward the office. As well as sessions, she runs the dungeon's social media accounts, and manages some of the booking schedules.

I love working here. It means I don't need to invest in my own equipment or rent on real estate. The dungeon is meticulously cleaned, deeply sterilised daily, and the furniture and fittings are regularly maintained for optimal safety for our high end clients.

I pop some pain killers in my mouth, swirl the liquid in my glass and down the pills with a mouthful of my martini. I jiggle my lovely tits in the mirror. My figure is looking spectacular in this well worn, tight, leather corset.

Grabbing my leather cap and leaning heavily on my cane, I tap my way toward the prison role play room.

Yes, twenty years throwing men around has had its ups and downs. The sadistic pleasure I take from this job also has its flip side. The arthritis, the joint pain, the stalkers and blackmailers.

Tonight's client is a CEO tech bro twat muffin named Gerard something or other. Not sure of the details, I've never asked him because he always pays upfront and he hasn't booked me for a conversational session yet.

Tonight he's paid handsomely for a high risk, heavy police interrogation scene. Hard impact, fear, intimidation, bruises and broken flesh is A-OK. Degradation, abuse, the whole nine. He loves me for my sadistic roleplay dialogue.

I yank open the door, and smile inwardly as he kneels, naked, nose to the cold concrete floor as I come in and close the door behind me. I ignore him as I make my way across the room to the prison desk next to the 'holding cells'. I check his intake consent form, checking over his medical conditions to make sure I play within his consensual limits. I note he has a recent shoulder injury, and make a mental note to avoid anything that may hurt him permanently.

I'm about fear and release in a safe space. Not long term injury and lawsuits.

This is one of my favourite rooms of the warehouse space. Heavy role play and corporal punishment is my favourite thing to do, and this room of the complex has everything I need for mock interrogations.

My pussy tingles as I think back to the last session I had with this man. I was riding an adrenaline high for days. He's sent money to my bank regularly since the first day he laid eyes on me.

He's devoted. Monogamous only to me like all the rest. My little piggy who also likes a Mommy, or a Headmistress, or a dirty cop.

Like today. I straighten my leather police cap and grab a folder from the stack on the large desktop. I walk toward him, the prop manilla folder only here for the small details. This is what high end clients pay for. Not only my innate talent, but for the small details. I wave the folder in front of his face.

"We have evidence! You're guilty!"

THWACK!

The whoosh of air as I throw it at his head, papers scattering in a dramatic arc across the room, fluttering to the floor. He whimpers, hands covering his head. He pisses himself on the floor.

"We have the evidence stacked against you, Mr Sutchins. Such a big man, taking advantage of all those innocent people. Robbing them of their life savings, their pensions! The boys are going to love you behind bars, oh yes they are. Well, it's lucky for you I ended up on your case ..."

I stifle a laugh as I stick the bottom of my cane under his chin, forcing him to look me in the eye. I make my expression stern. He does as I command, his eyes wide with fear.

Just how I like it.

"Look at me, worm," I snarl. "Do you think you're going to be walking out of here today without a few bruises?"

The session carries on, and my mind drifts back to the poor 6'4" man-child-idiot that I have tied up in his own room, in his sound proof bachelor pad, with the very same chains he hooked up to take advantage of young, drugged women. By now I'm sure he's pissed himself again, and he's likely clenching his butt cheeks together so he doesn't shit himself on his sexy satin black sheets.

Jerk.

Teaching him a lesson is my latest hobby, and I'm looking forward to getting back there to feed him later.

My focus returns to this man before me, whimpering, his cock in a cage, ring tight around his balls, heavy and full and an angry sad looking colour. I grab a wooden paddle covered in spikes, and beat the fuck out of his sack. As he chews on the frilly panties he recently removed from his sweaty ass crack, I laugh, and run a pinwheel and vampire gloves over him too.

A funny plan is forming for the smoke shadow fuckwit. And I need to talk to my very specific circle of smoke filled lungs to help with my sadistic plot.

[15]

KITTEN I'M FUCKED THE FIRST

"PLEASE DON'T SHIT, please don't shit, please don't shit."

I repeat my mantra like it's *Namafuckingstay*, as sweat drips over my eyes. Okay, not sweat, tears, this bitch is psycho.

Whatever is coming next, I know for sure it's not gonna be an acoustic rendition of *Kumbayah*.

This *R.E.S.P.E.C.T* song has been blasting for hours on repeat now, not one moment of silence, twelve hours straight at least. I get it. I'm a jerk. I should respect women more, yada yada. I've been alone for hours, and tears streak my cheeks because I cannot listen to this Respect song one more time without going insane. I want to die, this is tactical psyops, fucking warfare goddamn it. I play games, watch movies. I squeeze my butt cheeks together.

My arms are restrained, so I can't even cover my ears as the song grinds to its end and starts up immediately, I can only hope that my tears fill my ear canals so at least it's mildly dulled.

"Fuck my life," I groan.

My dick cries, trapped inside the woman's metal, and I need to piss again. I want to die. Her eyes crinkled at the corners come to mind, she is pretty.

My neighbours aren't disturbed by the noise that's driving me mad, of course, because of my awesome acoustic design skills. Why am I so good at everything I try?

So my neighbours can't hear my screams, and my online friends won't help cause none of them know where I live. And my family told me not to call again when I stole their stupid car.

Another trickle of fear finds its way up my throat, and I vomit the last bit of fluid left in my body. I cry and try to roll into a fetal position, unable to because of my chains, and I cringe as I squeeze my sphincter tightly.

Holding my turd turtle inside my body has been my only mission. Whatever those black pills were, they want to exit my body now. And surely she's coming back to let me go.

My triple monitors spark to life, and a video starts to

play. It's the same Plague Doctor from the party, and the same robotic voice starts to talk.

"Hello. Have you been making considered changes to your Masked Hero bullshit? How do you feel about consent today? Learned any lessons about treating women with respect?"

Respect.

The song plays three more times, and tears fall freely. Everything is numb. My body, my mind, my soul.

"Yes! Yes! I've learned my lesson! Respect women! I will from now on, I promise. Let me go!"

But the loud song starts up again and the tears fall as well.

I'm just cursing myself for falling for another unhinged — gorgeous — manic pixie dream girl. I should have known better. I'll be more careful next time. Maybe stick with the normal romance girls. My friends warned me, stay away from those dark romance girlies they said. They want you to chase them through the fucking forest with a gag in their mouth! Why didn't I listen to my friends? How did I get here?

Cause I'm tall, hung, and ripped, that's how I got here, and I fuck them exactly how they like it. All night long. My dick is huge, and they always come, and some of them even squirt. I'm the fucking king. My dick tries to throb through the cage, and I'm reminded that she's turned me into her bitch. My nuts are so squashed, I've never known pain like it.

This cunt of a blonde thing with her bedazzled everything. Kicking my door in and turning me to a captive, in my own damn apartment. Who does she think she is? I bet she just wants to fuck me like the rest of them. This is just some weird dark romance girl roleplay shit I haven't heard about yet. Those bitches are fucked.

[16]

MISTRESS CANE

"AND CAN you pick up my prescription for me? I sent the e-script to your phone. And if you find the time, you can start gluing the black and purple crystals onto the new inhalers if you get the chance. You know I love my sparkly inhalers!"

"Yes Mistress," comes the reply. "I will do that for you. I got some new diamonds and glue in the post last week that I'd like to test out."

"Good dog. See you later."

"The pleasure is all mine."

I hang up the phone from my pup and place it on my dressing table at the warehouse. The frames of lightbulbs surround my aging reflection, and I smile at myself.

I pinch my nipples and smile in the mirror. As I bite into one of the plump green olives from my drink, Goddess Paradox knocks on the door.

I smile up at her from my dressing table and wave her in. Her gold stiletto heels snake their way up her long, athletic legs.

"Hi, love," she says, breezing in and bending down to kiss me on both cheeks. "I got a couple of emails from the boss to send your way. It's a doozy, let me tell you."

I kiss her back and smile.

"Looking forward to it. I'm up to date with rent, so I don't know what he can have to bitch about."

"That's not why I'm here, though. I had dinner with Ember last night, and it looks as though there may be a few products coming on the market through her channels, if the club is interested. Nothing via the internet, though, we'll have to meet in private. Maybe you could try and coordinate the girls for a long weekend? Surely we all deserve a soak in the spa and a few bottles of wine? A dip in the lake?"

I look at her, brown eyes pleading. I've been promising a girls' getaway at the holiday house up the coast, and it seems that this is just the excuse we need.

I say, "Done. I'll let the pups know to pack my bags and get the cars ready. We can leave after work tomorrow night if you like. Be up there for the sunrise? Maybe even go for a dip in the ocean? The dogs can each drive a vehicle, which will get all of us up there, and we can chat on the way."

[17]

MISS MISERY

I CAN'T STOP THINKING about Smoke Shadow. He's been offline for a few days now, so all his groupies are wondering where he is. I see ripples of conversations as I scroll through the livestreams, whispers of "He's probably having an orgy," or "He's probably flying to Italy to fuck some hot chick over there." One room was even buzzing that he's been hired as an actor in a feature film. The rumours swirl. I miss his voice.

I despise that I can't break this cycle of being attracted to pretty sexy men with nothing between their ears. Why do I want to be ploughed by them?

I'm a smart woman, god damn it, so why can't I think about anything other than the way this dropkick's voice makes me tingle in all the right places? There are a million other women out there who love his smooth voice as much as I do. I know he's a player. And all I want him to do is wrap his big hands around my throat, and fuck me until I pass out with a huge grin spread across my face. He's a creep in every sense of the word, so why do I so desperately need him all to myself?

$$[\ 18 \ ]$$

KITTEN SADBOY

I open my eyes, head throbbing with a pain I've never felt. I don't know how many days I've been here, but I'm so thirsty.

I'm still chained, covered in my own fluids, but now I see someone has installed an oversized rodent water vessel while I've been asleep. I can reach over to lick it, and I suck on it desperately, feeling the water slide down my throat.

Once I've had my fill, I notice a brick of pet shop rodent feed, and dread fills me as I realise that this could be my only meal for the foreseeable future.

"Hey, baby, is that pussy looking to be taken care of tonight?"

I spin to see Paradox and Stitching, both standing in the bedroom doorway of Cane's beach house.

And by beach house, I mean a multi-million dollar house on Sydney's northern beaches.

We arrived in two cars and went for a dip as the sun rose. Beautiful morning.

Now, I raise my brows and take a step toward them both, sliding my arms around their waists, the scents of their skin and perfumes arousing my senses.

"Depends who's offering, and a little more details on how the taking care would be unfolding."

We all tumble into the bed together, tongues and fingers and legs everywhere.

Their softness fills my soul, and we connect between the sheets as we do in the dungeon.

[20]

MISTRESS CANE

EMBER DIVES into the infinity pool, and I watch as the water splashes against the hot tiles.

She does a lazy lap and pops up at the shallow end, lifting her toned arms out and leaning against the side of the pool.

"I think the shipment arrives next week, but it could be sooner. Keep our channels open. Banks would rather we take the females, you know how he is. He gets weird with perverted women. Doesn't like cleaning up that bullshit. Would rather women deal with their own freaks."

I scoff. "Yeah. I know how he is. Cocky prick. Anyway, I'll take whatever he has left over after his other clients are done. I know Dahlia can always take a few more rescue pets. The worst of the worst, you know. The ones that prison would be too good for."

She nods, smiling, before doing a duck dive and disappearing under the water again.

Good.

I need some more meat to keep Dahlia happy. That weird fucking doll thing she's creating is really taking shape.

She's a weirdo, but the best kind of weirdo to know.

Ember pops her perfect blonde head out of the pool again and rings her hair as she emerges up the steps, stark naked and glowing with vitality.

Better the devil you know than the devil you don't. That's what I always say.

Goddess Paradox emerges from the house, naked except for a golden belly chain and matching anklets. Her Afro hair is freshly shaved bald, Mistress Stitching's fine work. Paradox's long legs stretch across the tiles before springing her into a perfect, splashless dive into the deep end. She streaks down the pool underwater like a flash.

I fucking love my life.

MISERY JOURNAL OF NIGHTMARISH PROPORTIONS

The unholy, heathen diaspora.
A glimpse through the curtain of
insanity.
Your liver, your snout
Your soul.
I am it.
With a lowercase i, cannibal and
carnivorous.
One thousand words. Scare them off.
Meat for the taking.
It wasn't just a phase — the rebels.
Black sheep.
Scapegoats.
Outlaws.

The circle opens into a horseshoe.
Sovereign of the Dark

The circle opens into a horseshoe.
Sovereign of the Dark

[22]

SHE TURNED the music off about an hour ago, and the high pitched ringing in my ears is driving me insane.

A noise at my apartment's front door, I want to scream but I also don't want that she-devil anywhere near me. I couldn't keep the turtle at bay any longer, so now I'm laying in my shit, piss, and vomit, tears and blood.

I hear Little Miss Pepper Bitch before she gets to my room, and I know it's her, because I'm the only one with a set of keys, and I'm pretty sure she is now in possession of my keychain.

Because I'm still chained to my bed. Now I hear her chilling voice. Shit. She really is a great voice actor, she can project it well. Maybe even better than me. No, that's not possible, but she's good.

"Need the toilet, little kitten? Squeezing your little tushy cheeks together yet?"

Her laugh is sadistic. Two tall men walk into the room, both at least my height, if not taller. They're wearing matching midriff tops with the words HE/HIM/HOLE on the front. One is built like a brick shithouse, the other looks like some kind of blonde Hollywood action star. Shit, he's maybe even hotter than me, which is rare. My dick shrivels and my balls crawl inside my body.

Each man is weighed down under a pile of shopping bags, cartons, various cat stuff, and oh no, a bunch of pink clothes. The bronzed brick shithouse dude is wearing pink diamond stripper heels, and I feel dizzy. He walks better than most chicks can in heels that high.

"What's going on?" I mutter under my breath.

Pepper taps into the room behind the men, ignoring me and pointing around the room.

The men follow her, putting the stuff down. One of them sets up the cat litter in the corner, pouring in the moisture absorbing crystals. The other unpacks a bunch of sex toys and dress up clothes, the kind of stuff that cute little E-GIRLs wear.

"Oh shit," I mumble under my breath. Luckily she ignores me as the men do their tasks. Then, they both kneel at her feet, and I watch in horror as she lifts her boot up, showing them the scuffed sole, and each man takes their turn licking the dirt from the bottom.

"Thank you Mistress," they say in unison.

"Good dogs," she says to them as they stand up again. "You can stand guard at the door, but this Kitten here isn't going anywhere," she says, and giggles before turning to me.

The men stand one either side of my bedroom door in the military position, and I notice one of them has produced a Glock from somewhere.

Oh fuck.

She shakes her head at me.

"You've made a very stinky mess now, haven't you silly little baby? How am I going to hand you over to your new forever adoptive family, if you shit all over your lovely bed? No, no, we cannot be having that." Pain sears through my body. God knows how she's done it this time, but I'm paralyzed and forced to listen to her continue. "I train my foster pets with harsh methods, but you'd best believe you will be fully housetrained and neutered before I hand you over, be sure of that!"

The sweat is dripping in rivers off every part of my body, as her words sink in. And I groan as my cock nudges against the harsh steel. She's magically forcing my dick to harden with her voice alone, even though I don't want to be horny now. She's edging me. Torturing me.

She's just a dumb fucking —"

Zap zap zap.

Fuck, she's tasered me again, my limbs contract and flex as she takes me out.

[23]

MISTRESS CANE

I was sick of dealing with his crusty bleeding face looking at me anymore, so I casually tasered him; knocked him out good and proper so I could get some rearranging done in his new Babygirl pink Kitten house.

While he was out, I jerked him to a rigid hard on, which lets face it, wasn't difficult. He is a virile young specimen, I'll give him that. And if I didn't have greater, more noble plans for this shithead, I'd keep him for myself. Add him to my pack.

But no, for my greater plans I set about working quickly, and jerked his cock while he was out. Without his consent, because he doesn't believe in consent, I heard him. So I set his dick in a cast.

As Jamoa packs away the craft supplies I used for the cast, he chuckles. He knows what I have in plan for this at a later date. He's seen this trick before.

In past experience, I've found the cast of his very own manhood will come in handy later when it comes time to teach him the real lesson about consent. To be honest, with this vain prick, I'm surprised he's not selling dildos in the shape of his own tattooed cock.

I get the pupcakes to help me rip out all his black furnishings and shit that gives him the illusion of alpha male, and have them drill in some new pink furniture and shelves with adorable, uwu decorations. With his Shadow Daddy vibes stripped, we redecorate with a nice little pink rug on the floor, and some pink bows for decoration.

Hemschris sets up a single wardrobe rack, and hangs up Kitten's new array of clothes. A pretty pink leather harness, some pink kitten ears, and before I leave, I'll be inserting a training kitten tail plug up his ass.

I thought about waking him up to make him clean up his bodily fluids mess, but decided that it's quicker if I just get the boys to help me do a change of his bed, popping on the fresh My Little Pony blanket and a cute little water fountain that gurgles fresh water out. Cats love that shit, apparently. I also leave him a ball of string to play with.

Jamoa unhook three of his limbs, so from now on he will have access to move about his designated pet quarters. I need to teach him basic toilet training.

I slap him on the cheek repeatedly, and when he wakes up, he's going to have some tasks that he will need to do for his new training Mistress.

"Hang the chart on the wall over there please Jamoa, right where he can see it from every angle his chain allows him to reach. He needs to be housebroken, doesn't he? Silly little thing. Oh, and open that new shock collar, and put it on him, we can test it out."

The boys laugh along with me, and go about getting everything ready, as Kitten's eyes widen as I sit back in a chair and light up a joint.

"This is fun, isn't it?" I ask him. "You're learning to stay quiet aren't you? Good boy. This is my favourite sport you know, knocking predatory losers down a few rungs. Breaking them and rebuilding them to an asset to society, rather than the liability you are."

My guard dogs nod along in silence, smiling at me with their hungry gaze. They hate predators, and as much as I know both of these guys would love to just put a bullet in his skull and be done with it, for the way he's treated women in the past, I know they both prefer to watch me knock sense into him over a prolonged period of time.

My pussy tingles again, as I plan exactly how I want Jamoa and Hemschris to eat me out when we get home after this little trip to feed and water my latest pet.

I'm a great pet owner. These two guard dogs have experienced my training and handling, they know exactly how to please their mistress with their fingers and tongues alone. And no one can accuse me of mistreating my pets.

Sure, I'll let them wallow like a pig in their shit for a few hours, but that's only to teach them a lesson. Especially when they're as cocky as this fuckwit.

And perhaps some of my training techniques could be considered **'unethical', 'inhuman,'** *and* **'torture.'**

I don't agree.

The way creeps like this have the audacity to prey on young women. Young women, mind you, without fully formed frontal lobes.

Wimps. With their fucking Little Lamb, Little Prey, Little Toxic Doll.

I shudder.

"Oh look, he's realising he's only attached by his ankle." This little moment buoys my mood. "Oh, Jamoa my filthy little pup, be a dear grab your Mistress that new spray bottle? And, do you need to take a leak after the drink you had in the car?"

"Yes Mistress," he replies.

I zap the shock collar, and watch as the Kitten flails about.

I watch his little display as I laugh, and Jamoa hands me

the empty spray bottle he picked up at the hardware store, and I unscrew the lid as he unzips his fly.

"Fill this for me will you, Pupcake? I'll get you a *pup cup* on the way home after this."

"Of course Mistress," Jamoa says. "Can I have sprinkles and marshmallows?"

"Anything you want, babycakes. You know, you're my right hand dawwg."

I lick my lips and watch as this Titan unfurls his giant brown cock and pisses neatly into the bottle. He gives his dick a double shake and tap for good measure before handing it back to me. I screw the lid on, and smile as my new Kitten comes to his stupid senses.

"Good morning Kitten. You'll see I've redecorated a little for you, put a few rules up on the walls, installed your new toilet, and now I'm going to teach you a lesson. No more pissing in the bed."

I spray him in the face with urine, until it's dripping off his eyelashes and his face is soaked. Then, I shock his collar again.

"Now, bend over."

He bends over and I shove the kitten butt plug up his ass with no lube.

He screams bloody murder, but I just turn my back and say over my shoulder, "Behave yourself, and I'll see you tomorrow Little Kitten." Heading toward the door, and without looking back, I add, "Come on boys, I think I'd like my toes licked tonight."

I grab my cane, pain shooting through my back as I get out of the chair again, and swing this dipshit's keychain around in a circle, enjoying the terror in his eyes, before leaning on my stick, and making my way toward the door.

"Oh and kitten, my friends and I are arranging an event for you to apologise directly to your sexual assault victims. Aren't we boys?"

My loyal K9 guard pups say in unison, "Yes Mistress."

Their voices darker and sexier than this pathetic Kitten's could ever hope to be. "Good boys. You've pleased your Mistress. Oh, and Kitten, if you want to hang yourself with that ball of string be my guest. I don't really care if I have to get my pups to take the trash out if we come back to a crime scene here tomorrow."

I make sure I'm laughing all the way down his long corridor, and all the way out his apartment door. Hemschris extends a stable arm to me as we make our way back to the car.

I fucking love my life.

[24]
RATTY THE THIRD

THE GRATING sound of metal and rock startles me from sleep, and my eyes burn as the daylight fills my prison well.

Yes.

Well, not cell. She threw me down a well.

Callsign Miss Misery.

My mouth is dry, parched, and my itchy skin is driving me insane. I don't know what these little flying bugs are, some kind of microscopic fly, but their bites make me scratch myself raw.

I watch in fear as a plastic bag lands near my feet with a thud.

The sinister voice calls from above.

"You'd better ration bitch. The crows are watching, but I don't know when we'll be back to feed you next. Hope there's lots of sewer water down there, cause without it, you've got about three days, give or take."

The grate slides closed above me again, and I pull the cardboard around my raw flesh tighter, my damp t-shirt ragged and stinking like death.

All I have to look forward to is slipping into nightmares so I can escape this living hell.

I know this is where I'm going to die.

The only question I have left now is when?

[25]

MISS MISERY

THE BLACK GAME buttons are worn out from playing this damn new game on my old handheld. I should pop a new console onto my wishlist. A paypig will get it for me and thank me for the honour of making my day a little brighter. It's the least he can fucking do.

I continue running around this new game with my cutesy gamer friends, planting strawberries and tending to my electric sheep in my cyber farm.

The audiobook of Neuromancer plays on the speakers as I chat with my girlfriends about random bullshit, laughing and drinking together. Chomping snacks and laughing late into the night.

It's nice to have had a break from Callsign Shadow Daddy. It was good that his channel disappeared. I needed to go cold turkey on that motherfucker. My stalking obsession was so bad it was affecting my quality of life.

I just want to be left alone, take care of my real pets and my electric pets, and that's good enough for me. I keep my circle small, but those who are allowed into my day-to-day existence are all there for a reason. They add something to my quality of life, don't detract from it.

With my besties, I don't feel like shit after I say goodbye to them. I look forward to talking to them again; they're not a drain.

I get up to make a drink, take a slash, and water my little succulent babies. Playfully, a hungry Venus flytrap snaps my fingertips when I stick a finger in.

Scanning my monitors in my gaming corner, I flop back. Looking for my gamer friends, I scroll through endless boring servers. Someone will read a nighttime, after-hours, spicy book for us to listen to together. While we jerk ourselves in surround sound. When we drink and smoke and unleash mayhem. I pop into some slutty audio channels, and the creepy dudes growling into the microphone make my skin crawl. I shudder, flashing back to the way my ex used to growl those disgusting things in my ears as he took advantage of me.

Over. and Over. and Over.

Call sign fuckwits with their pretty little masks and their pretty mascara. Ice-blue eyes. Shady intent lurking behind the long lashes and gravelly voices. Luring young women to their future trauma therapy. Their future EMDR and CPTSD diagnoses.

Creepy fuckers. Fucking Shadow Daddies and Callsign Twatwaffles.

MESSAGE FROM CYBERQUEEN.

```
HEY BITCH, ARE YOU ROTTING
IN BED?

                    HOW'D YOU KNOW?

...
I TRACK YOUR PHONE
LOCATION, DUH.

                          OH YEAH

GET DRESSED. I'M ON MY WAY
TO GET YOU. WE'RE GOING FOR
A DRINK. NO BIGGIE, NO
DRESSUPS. JUST A QUICK
CATCH UP.

                Ugh. ok. if i must.
```

I drag myself out of bed and run a brush through my hair. Throwing a studded leather jacket on, I say goodbye to my pets and lock the door behind me.

Out on the street, I light a cigarette as I wait for my friend's car to come around the corner. Puffing smoke into the night sky, I glance up at the fresh new moon and think about how my dreams are coming to fruition.

I hold the cigarette in my mouth as I crack my knuckles and then my neck.

[26]

KITTEN SILLYSPHINCTER

Today, Mistress Cane's psyops song of choice has been You Outta Know by Alanis Morissette. She announced it like a radio presenter introducing it on the air waves. I hadn't heard it before, and the first time I heard it I thought it was catchy.

By hour four I was crying. She laughed at me relentlessly over my computer, and sang along over my speakers, bullying me. Taunting me.

"If I have to shove some feminism down that pretty throat, we can do it this way with music, or I can come over there right now and show you in person!" she'd said. "I'll be bringing my sounding kit."

I shut up for a while after that. By hour sixteen of that song on repeat at an earpiercing decibel. I was begging her to shoot me in the face and put me out of my misery.

I turn my head and re-read her latest 'sign' on the wall.

. . .

Be nice to all women.

Treat all humans with respect.

Now, you're going to repair the damage you've done to the community. You're going to get together with all your mods and apologise to your victims. Each one will receive a heartfelt apology in her inbox from you. And once that is sent, you will never contact them again.

I have left you a small laptop — don't worry, you can't get on the net

Get this homework done or you may not last the next week.

They can barely remember you, Little Kitten, sorry, Callsign Smoke Knob Jockey. You can shove your microphone up your fucking ass.

Time passes in a blur of different songs on repeat, and replays of every dumb thing I've ever said to a woman, playing over and over all night. Interspersed with the times she radios in some way, and blares her ridicule and bullying tactics at me.

This bitch is smart. I wouldn't be surprised if she's some ex high ranking military boss of some description.

I think back to various stupid shit I've done over the years. Like at that party in high school, when I lit my farts on fire. The times we jumped off the roof on a BMX and landed in the pool. Then at the hospital.

I sink into a horrible depression. A fucking cone and a Monster would be fucking good right now. She keeps my apartment dark, like a casino, so I never know what time it is.

And various voices, both anonymous, and her, laugh and taunt me relentlessly. She's like a fucking chainsaw, waking me up after every hour. Sleep deprivation is real, the CIA knew what they were doing.

I cry and lick the water she's left in a giant oversized hamster water bottle next to my head. I'm still tied up in my chains.

"Hello Kitten. This anonymous woman is here to seek revenge on the way you treated her. You will take it like a man, because you're Callsign Smoke Shadow Daddy. No one can own you. You think you can't be owned? Surprise cock head! My sexy friend here is about to edge you until you spurt, and you're going to hate every fucking second of it."

The silent woman dressed head to toe in leather, full hood too, strides over, and pulls me up by my neck. In her hand is a thick leather paddle, covered with long metal studs.

She throws me against the wall, and in a low seductive voice commands, "Bend over."

I do as she says, touching my toes, ass in the air in fucking down dog. I'm nothing but a dog, I get it. Funny haha. I'm bracing for the pain of the thrashing I know is about to rain down on me. My butt cheeks clench tightly at the anticipated sting. The pain of my flesh searing in bleeding strips off my ass.

This is what happens now. Every day. Anonymous, masked women are brought over, and allowed to unleash their revenge upon me. A kind of, 'torture him as much as you feel he deserves' kind of arrangement. And these goth baddies are much more crazy than I anticipated. I always saw them as my prey, but they fucked that idea up its ass.

[27]

MISTRESS CANE

JAMOA's long brown locks are covered in suds, as he sits naked in a bubble bath, and I massage his hair in shampoo.

"Oh, this is nice, isn't it my little Pup Cup?"

He hums, "Mmmm, very nice thank you Mistress."

I see his cock bobbing up out of the suds, as he leans back, eyes closed, stupid long lashes laying across his cheeks.

I love these moments of care with my precious boys.

"You're such a sweet Mistress," he says. A little happy growl escapes him, as my fingers press into his favourite pressure points in the base of his skull.

"Good boy," I purr, as I continue to massage his scalp. "Now, eyes on me."

131

He turns to lean his angular chin on the rim of the porcelain bath, and watches adoringly as I disrobe, and do a couple of spins, before I hobble toward the bath, and slide in beside him.

He wraps me in his arms, and his warmth and security surround me.

[28]

KITTEN POOPYFACE THE FIFTH

My hand aches as I hand write my lines over and over for Mistress Cane. Filling books.

CONSENT MATTERS.
SAFE WORDS ARE THERE FOR A
PURPOSE.
DON'T STEP OVER BOUNDARIES

My leg shakes over and over, because I can't stim out my facehole anymore, it comes out as twitches in my legs.

I hunch over my paper, like in a classroom, writing over and over. The cramp takes over my hand and I drop my pen, my eyes flicker up to meet hers in case she's going to shock me with the collar, or worse, the fucking taser again.

She's scrolling on her phone and drinking coffee, as her tall scary minion guard dogs go about cleaning my room and taking care of the aroma. She still gets very mad when my shit stinks. Which is every fucking day, lets be real.

"Mistress, may I speak, please?"

She glares at me.

"What is it, fuckface?" she asks with a bored sigh.

"What's in those black pills you shove down my neck every day?"

It's been bothering me. A lot.

Her shrill laugh makes me jump involuntarily. Everything freaks me out these days. I can never anticipate her next insane chess move. Every fucking time she comes here, she shoves those giant black horse pills down my flesh pipe, and my stomach stabs with cramps as I worry about every single chemical she's probably shoved in my body. I need to shit. Again. She's strategic, and the black pebble shit I've been doing for the last week is scaring me.

I'm finally getting used to using the humiliating kitty litter box, so I have to see every single little black lump that I squeeze out my ass. She's still laughing, slapping her knee. She pulls a glittery inhaler out of her bra, shakes, puffs, and returns it.

Finally she calms her hysterics enough to smile at me with her frightening eyes. The way she looks at me is as though I'm a dumb toddler.

She says, "You're such a fucking idiot, you know that, right? Surely someone other than me has told you that before."

I groan as another cramp tears through my gut.

"It's fucking charcoal and iron tablets, you dipshit. I look after my pets; they're keeping you healthy. Just wanted to fuck with your head, like you fucked with all those women."

I don't say anything, because there is no point. She's given me freedom today. Only one ankle is chained, which means I can move about the room and use my kitty litter like the good boy I am. I shake my hand and finish my lines. Today I'm learning Romanian and French phrases, ones that show respect and admiration to women. She has given me a bookshelf stacked with books on human rights and feminism to study.

Without warning, the now familiar spark of electricity surges around my neck as she shocks my collar from the remote on the table beside her. My brain fries, and tears leak from my eyes.

The searing pain passes, and I look down at my tear-streaked, blue-lined exercise book, as I continue my page after annoying fucking page of lines.

I want to scream, 'You're such a fucking bitch!'

But sadly, I know better now. My tears run down my nose and drip onto the paper, and I don't bother wiping them away.

I rarely do these days. I'm her slave, well and truly. My days are filled with her stupid bullshit rules on the wall, and getting dressed up in frilly kitten ears and stupid pink bras and lingerie.

She makes it her priority to check in on me at least once a day, to spend time here, leering at me. Bullying me. Teaching me her stupid lessons. I want to choke her, my thumbs pressing into her skinny neck until life leaves her eyes.

I want to kill her, but I keep my mouth shut; I'm learning. I'm a good boy. A good kitten. A good little fucking princess, and I cringe as I listen to the sound of her sadistic laughter. The ever-looming presence of the bulky ex-military men snooping silently about my house. Their leather holsters and multiple weapons are always out and proudly on display for me.

I'm well and truly fucked.

[29]

MISTRESS CANE

"I'm nervous," Dahlia says as we drive through the city streets. Leafy Sydney suburbs turn into the Harbour Bridge, and turn into stacks of concrete dominos all ready to topple each other over.

I nod and she continues speaking quietly, almost as though to herself.

"I can't believe it's all finally coming into place. All these dreams I've had for decades. I'm so excited to teach this specific cuck-head the need for a fucking safeword. To discuss consent and boundaries and the importance of not drugging and raping innocent women. Despite what they wear or read or say. He needs to learn some more lessons. I'm ready to teach him a fucking lesson; rip him a gaping new asshole, ready for what's to come at Halloween. And I'm going to love every second of it."

I smirk at her, pride swelling in my heart at how far this Mistress has come from the time I met her all those years ago. She was but a shadow of the woman who sits next to me, fully in her power, a perfect blend of feminine and masculine. Shadow and light. Submissive and dominant. She's a goddess unto herself. Just like me.

"I can't wait to watch this show," I say to her, my voice full of pride.

Jamoa is at the wheel, snickering. Hemschris is riding shotgun, both of them probably hard at the thought of what's to come. My pussy is still throbbing from their mouths. We're all voyeurs, let's face it. And the chance to watch two sexy people fuck, is too good an opportunity to pass up on a lazy Tuesday afternoon.

"No need to be nervous honey, and I get the anger. He's a prick, he always will be. He'll never change. He will never treat women with respect. You're in full control of this, I told you. If it all goes to shit, Hemschris will put a bullet in his head and feed him to the crocs. You've got this."

I reach across and take her cold hand in mine, giving it a tight squeeze.

"Thanks Mistress. For your kindness and support. For your unconditional friendship and love, for getting this man ready for me, and allowing me to pop another cherry."

She smiles at me then looks out the window at the city whizzing by, and I pretend not to see the glistening of poignant tears in her eyes, as I keep hold of her hand.

"I remember that feeling. The nerves of going out on your own. The responsibility that comes with this line of work. But I have faith in you, and I'd trust you with my life. You've alchemised so much in the last four years, and you don't need me any longer. Fly, spread your wings, find the people who make your heart sing."

I look away from her as Jamoa parks my car in the underground carpark of Kitten's apartment block and when the car rolls to a stop, the guard dogs hop out and open our doors for us with a smile.

I think we're all excited for today. The pups carry our bags upstairs, and by the time Jamoa opens the kitten's front door, I think we're all chomping at the bit to watch this live sex show.

Before we head to his bedroom set for the show, Dahlia zips on her hood. She's chosen to remain anonymous with this Kitten, for now. She's going to do her big reveal when she celebrates her move into her brand new private dungeon in the suburbs. She's been saving for this move for years, she's budgeted and planned all the decorating and furniture down to pinterest boards, suppliers details and finally it's all coming to fruition. Dahlia seems to have a weird crush on this stinking creature, some weird and twisted obsession that I don't understand. I don't get it, I've kicked a thousand men like this one, he's nothing special.

Dahlia and I grin at each other as we follow Jamoa down the hall, his pretty heels click clacking along with our own, with the platforms it raises him up to almost 7 '1, and I smile at the little things that make us happy.

We arrive at his stupid completely soundproofed bedroom, and gaze upon his poor little setup. He's got a cat buttplug hanging out his bootyhole, and he's absolutely fucking miserable.

He glares at us all with a scowl that deserves a fucking shiny gold award, and I laugh at his obvious displeasure and fear.

"Hello Little Kitten, Mommy's home! Did you miss me?" I ask in yet another voice he's never heard before. Or maybe he has as I was doing my own research on him, months before I kicked him in his empty chest and taught him his very first lesson on judging a book by its cover, or, a voice actor by his fry.

"Hello, Mistress," he replies. "I missed you, how may I be of service?"

He's glaring at us, that lovely fear standing guard in his pretty blue eyes. I grab a pink leather paddle from nearby, and raise it.

"I think I'd like to see you get fucked up the ass with an exact replica of your huge fucking cock. Nice tattoo by the way. I gave you a free handy when I knocked you out on one of my care trips to change your litter. A few weeks ago. Sorry you missed it, it was fun for me, anyway." I love saying shit like this to him.

He's finally learning his lesson.

Kitten stands up from his pink bed, chains jangling as he shuffles to kneel on his pretty shag pile, heart shaped, pink rug, dipping his hands and nose to the floor.

"Do you remember Mistress Dahlia, pet? She will be leading your lesson today, it's a very special day for you little boy. She's going to pop your cherry, aren't you lucky?"

His head snaps up, and his eyes dart between the four of us standing above him.

Mistress Dahlia looks absolutely hot as fuck, in her head to toe latex number, her hood slick on her face, and the two white ponytails of hair that fall down her back from the top of the hood. The cut outs allow us to see her eyes and mouth.

"You're fucked, aren't you my little ashtray?" I say to the manchild in his stupid pink thong.

Dahlia can't help laughing at the pathetic scene before her, and the sound of her joy fills me with my own warped sense of happiness.

"Yes Mistress," Kitten says, as he lowers his nose back to

the floor. "I'm extremely fucked from the looks of things."

His voice is muffled as he curls into a ball, probably anticipating another kicking.

Dahlia steps forward.

"Sit on your ankles, show me that cock."

He sits up, his cock semi rigid, trapped in his cage.

"I have plenty of footage of you spouting your nonsense on a public forum about how women don't need safewords. It's funny you know, some may call me mainstream in my thinking, but I think consent always matters. Everywhere. And in every situation. And, you know what you've said and done, and you know what's coming. And you know you deserve it, don't you, Kitten?"

[30]

KITTEN AWAKENING CHERRYPIP

MISTRESS CANE and Mistress Dahlia laugh openly at me, from behind their sexy latex hoods, as those huge watch dog motherfuckers stand guard behind them with their Glocks and jujitsu moves.

Something about Mistress Dahlia seems familiar, but I can't place it. Maybe it was her voice that taunted me some of those long nights I was listening to the same song on repeat for days on end. That time is kind of blurred into one long nightmare at this point.

Kinda wishing I'd taken a few classes in self defence before now. All that time was wasted lifting weights and jerking it in the mirror. Maybe if I'd actually gone to a few martial arts classes, I wouldn't be in this fucking predicament.

If I ever get out of this shitshow alive, I'm going to start training.

These hitman motherfuckers are just watching me with their neutral gaze, waiting for me to fuck up somehow. Chomping at the bit to kill me, or at the very least, rip a few toes off.

I shudder at the thought.

The dumb bitch says, "Jamoa, please step forward, and get the cat food tin for me. The salmon jelly one, I think that's his favourite flavour."

I watch as the hulking seven foot, bronzed god steps into the light. I cannot tear my eyeballs away from his long flowing, sunbleached hair. He's in a crop top with the bedazzled pink words stating, "Mistress Cane's Whore," on the front.

He moves to crack a pink labelled tin of Ocean Flavour catfood and as he turns, I notice on the back it says, "Slut Pup Cup," and my fear ramps up an octave.

Now I stare at his giant sparkly stripper heels, as he waits for the tiny blonde woman to give him his next order. Goosebumps spread, because I've come to realise that this little crazy Karen that hobbles around on a fucking cane is some kind of mob boss. She has an unknown cult of psychotic lunatics at the combat ready to do her unhinged, very fucking dark, bidding.

And for some unholy reason, I've ended up at the top of her shitlist. And I can't blast my way out of this strategically like I shoot my way out of a hoard of zombies.

What I wouldn't give to go back a few months, I'd stop fucking with girls on the internet. I'd focus more on myself, and less on what they all think of me. I can't breathe, gasping and choking oxygen into my lungs. The collar is hard around my throat.

And the fear ramps up now, because Mistress Dahlia comes over and shows me a little silver key, and bends to touch the metal cage holding my dick inside.

A surge of blood rushes to the place her soft fingers touched, and she releases me from the god forsaken cage. Her sexy tits are right in my face.

My cock throbs again, growing harder, and I groan, a tear rolling down my face, because she's about to do something to me, and my cock is going to be hard the entire time.

I don't know if I'm hallucinating, but that tall guy is wearing sparkly stripper heels again, and I think out of everything, that's what terrifies me the most.

I've fallen into some bad acid trip, that's it. That's what the pills are somehow. She's drugging me like I drugged those girls I met online, and I don't know how to wake up this horror film nightmare.

"Get that gorgeous sword out for your Mistress please Jamoa, and smear some of that delicious cat paste all over it. Make sure to get it all up under your balls, and your ass. Our sweet little kitten here is about to learn a small lesson about consent. He has never observed the need for safe words, so it seems from the receipts, emails, and hand on heart testimonies. But don't worry everyone, he doesn't get a safeword, not yet. He hasn't earned that privilege. And before you try and say, 'I always use safewords,' I call bullshit my Little Fucking Kitten. And so do the many young women — interestingly all 21 — they say otherwise. They say they came over to your little pad, and had a few drinks, and then passed out, only to wake up the next morning with no recollection of the previous night. And then porn turned up starring them. And you played your little blackmail routine with them all, they lovingly licked your knob on and on."

My hearing phases in and out. She knows about it all. All that shit on my hard drives, she's got it all. She carries on, shouting now.

"Fuck you really are a little creep, and you're lucky my gorgeous guard dog here is offering you the privilege of sucking his ginormous cock, rather than him strangling you with his firm thighs!"

She emphasises her speech, as she presses her fingernails into Jamoa's now naked and muscular as fuck thighs.

I'm pretty sure this is it for me. I'm about to die. All visions of every girl I've fucked and scammed and blackmailed rushes through my head. This monster of a man wearing high heels, being bossed around by a little devil woman is going to choke me to death with his ginormous cock, and it's even bigger than mine, if that's possible.

The revolting scent of catfood jelly wafts around my room. I gag, swallowing bile and heartburn watching the giant freak smearing it all over his cock.

Oh, holy fuck.

He's laughing like the fucking joker as he smears it under his hairy ballsack and shaft and walks toward me. I don't move, because why bother at this point?

The two glossy latex women have taken a seat and are both recording on their phones, giggling as this literal god leans down to take my head in his giant hand, gripping my hair and yoinking my neck back.

This hulk is tossing me around like his plaything.

"Broseph! You'd better stretch that pretty mouth open real wide now, cause I love sloppy blowies. No teeth now, old Little Smokey Mask!"

I close my eyes against the pain, and the knowing of what is about to come. Literally. I heave and can't stop myself from vomiting out my nose, fish finally overwhelming me.

Jamoa jumps back, laughing, his heels missing the splattery chunks of mushed industrial scale fishery scraps that cascade in pinks and browns from my mouth, and the two evil step bitches howling with glee at my doom.

The scary dude continues his threats.

"You'd better sit yourself down bitch, cause God herself is sick of your ass. I've been waiting for this blowie all day, I even skipped my morning jerk off. And now your mouth is mine. You can call me Mommy."

The world slows down and begins to spin like some bullshit ayahuasca or mushroom trip. I feel his giant brown dong find its way into my mouth and nudges smoothly straight past my gag reflexes.

My catfood dinner from earlier comes up again and splashes out my mouth like a projectile volcano.

"Oh, bitch. Clean that shit up. I'm not doing it."

He grips my head and forces me to lick every last drop of my vomit off his catfood smothered hairy ballsack.

I vomit again, and the cycle repeats, until he begins fucking my face like he's mad at it.

And I rise above my body, and watch from a distance.

I want to die. I can't take this anymore.

[31]

MISTRESS DAHLIA

MISTRESS CANE PULLS her sparkly inhaler out and takes four puffs, before slipping it away and continuing to laugh.

"Oh, Jamoa, you're so funny. Wake him up, don't let him pass out. He doesn't get out of a good stinky face fuck that easily. He has to experience it all first hand."

We continue to laugh together, recording the spectacle on our phones as evidence for later.

To continue blackmailing this silly twatwaffle.

Watching the catfood blow job has been entertaining, but now it's time to hose him off and pop his gaping journey cherry with an exact replica of his own giant schlong.

"How do you feel about consent now, Little Kitten Smoke Shadow Daddy? Are you ready to sit back, spread your thighs and hold your cheeks apart, and relax for Mistress?" I ask smoothly, with yet another sultry English accent he's never heard before.

I strap on my pale pink leather harness and slip in the giant silicone dong.

"No lube for you Kitty cat. You never brought any with you to the parties. The birds told me. Did you bring a condom? Would you like one now? Do you know what diseases Jamoa has over there? You're a cockhead!"

I cackle as my core begins to tingle, and I rub my clit through my shiny latex pants.

[32]

KITTEN STINKYFACE VOLCANOBUTT

THE BANSHEES ARE SCREECHING with laughter as Dahlia
drags me by the hair to my giant bed, now covered in
Hello Kitty bedding, and shoves my neck hard in the
stocks. As I'm coughing, she nimbly and efficiently locks
my head and arms in the bed, and then hoists my back
end up exactly where she wants it. Locks a spreader bar
between my ankles and chains it to the bottom of
the bed.

To the fucking chains I installed for myself.

Fuck my life.

"No KY for you, baby cakes," she says. "But how do you
feel about salmon jelly?

Lining up an exact replica of my own penis, which was
jerked out of me without my consent, she shoves the
pink cat food dong, every single, godawful inch of it,
straight up my ass. She's even gone to the detail of

having eight barbells inserted into the dildo, so I feel every, ass ripping, inch of what I've dealt up to women in gutters and behind garbage bins.

I howl, she is wordless but groaning with sadistic glee. I hear giggles and laughter, tittering and knee slapping at the pleasure of witnessing this ridiculous spectacle.

And they all had a hand in it, those militant dudes, the little blonde witch, and this fucking latex bitch, cackling with glee as she reams me.

My insides shred out with her every rough thrust, she's stronger than she looks, that's for sure, as she fucks me so hard I can't hear my own howls. I squeeze my insides hard against the onslaught, but I'm bound head down ass up, and she will never let up. Not until she's happy.

"Ooh, you're a girthy boy, aren't you Kitten Sparkles?" she coos at my back as she takes me like her little bitch.

Tears drip into my snot, and drip down the end of my bed, as echoes of her words ring in my mind along with the feminist songs Cane has been sending me crazy with all these dark and unnerving long days nights weeks months. I have no idea how long I've been here, it's just a nightmare.

I cannot with these masked bitches and feral guard dog hitmen.

Who do they think they are?

Who are they?

"You're a piece of shit," a man calls from the pink sparkly cuck chair they've set up in the corner of my bachelor master bedroom.

"Don't you know who I am?" I whisper.

I'm Callsign Smoke Shadow Daddy. I can make you come with my voice alone.

But now, all my voice is doing is shredding my vocal cords, as my desperate cries fall on my soundproofed apartment.

No one is coming for me.

My promises are empty, my words are lies. And that's why no one is coming to save me.

I'm a piece of shit, being fucked up the ass with my own dick.

I'm fucking pathetic. And my ass stinks like catfood.

"OOgie boogie! Happy Halloween bitch!" she says, as she finally shoves me so far into the stocks that my oxygen cuts off and the blackness fucks my ass.

[33]

MISTRESS CANE

THE LOVELY MORNING IS BRIGHT, and I'm finally in my sundress in the bush. Both the pupcakes have brought me to a lovely secluded location, where they've both stripped down, and we are all frollicking in the ferns.

I seize the opportunity, and have allowed Hemschris to take me in a rare moment, and he's fucking me up against a tree.

I'm into it, my pussy swallowing up his cock from behind, and as he thrusts hard, he shouts out, "That's it, take it you fucking whore."

Without warning, I crack my elbow to his nose, and blood spurts in a gush. In the seconds it takes him to slump backward and cover his bleeding face, I have unholstered and aimed my pink bedazzled gun at him.

Shoving it into his face hole, his eyes are squeezed tight

and he sits as still as a stone, waiting for me to serve up whatever is coming to him.

I smile as I watch the blood drip deliciously down his handsome and rugged face.

"Change of plans, WHORE," I growl at Hemschris, who still has his eyes squeezed tight. "Don't forget who the fucking CUP is in this pup cup scenario."

He knows I could shoot him at any moment, and that thought keeps his dick hard. He loves this shit. He asks for it, really.

But I can see him regretting that slip of the tongue.

"You're lucky I didn't cut your tongue off right now." I force him to bite the muzzle of the gun, before I remove it and shout, "Jamoa, fuck him up the ass however feral way you like. I don't give a damn about his booty hole at this point."

I bend to lick the blood from Hemschris's face, before replacing my gun in its leather holster, and wriggling back into my lace panties. I strip out of the dress and throw it at Hemschris.

"Put that on, now you can get railed in a sundress."

I laugh as Hemschris struggles his way into my tiny dress, as Jamoa lifts him off the ground with a whoop. He wrestles him back to the earth with a thump. He instantly wraps his legs around Hemschris's neck in one swift motion, the lust in his eyes at the opportunity before him. Flipping him over, and nudging his cock in its rightful place.

"Nice," I whisper to myself, and I grab my cane.

Pushing myself up to stand I watch as my lovely mutts fuck each other, their groans and hot, fast breath excites my lust, and I hobble across with pain searing through my joints, to the table. Lifting a giant red wobbling mountain of jelly, with cherries and icecubes, and I throw the whole thing over them and watch as it slides between their rippling muscles, and I giggle.

Dahlia is sitting in a camping chair, off to the side, watching my boys play with each other, her manicured fingers dipping between her open thighs. She rubs circles on her clit with one hand, and sips champagne with the other. Sucking her foot is a spec of dirt in a leather hood. I don't know who it is, and I don't give a fuck. He's there as her foot stool, or ashtray.

I watch as she pulls her toe out of his mouth, and kicks him in the nose.

"Open," she purrs.

He obediently opens his mouth, and she ashes her long menthol cigarette into it. Once she's done, and reclines again, he closes his mouth and swallows. Without a word, he lays down on the floor with his mouth open and erection nudging against the steel cage. She stands up on top of him, her balance on those six inch heels atop his muscular, tattooed body, is to behold.

"Your balance is perfect, you'd make a great runway model, you know. Ever thought about that?"

She scoffs. "Bit short for that thanks. I'm quite happy here, watching, and stepping on my new rug. Do you like it? I'm seeing if it is to my taste before I commit to rescuing it. You know how it is. I need a new ashtray and footstool and a multipurpose piece of furniture.

[34]

KITTEN ASHTRAYBUTT (NOTHING SPECIAL VERSION)

THE GOD-AWFUL SOUND of my testicles being kicked into my brain only amplifies the excruciating throb between my legs.

I cannot breathe, cannot scream, can't even remember my name, as I roll around pathetically on the floor of this terrifying, fully equipped dungeon, fortress, mansion of the damned.

I'm not sure if this is better than hell.

My soul escapes my body through my scrotum, as I wriggle on the floor like the worm I apparently am now. The pain is incomparable. I'm owned by this bitch and her gaggle of shady friends.

My body parts are searing after being obliterated by Mistress Dahlia's sexy leather thigh-high boots.

My poor cock throbs without my brain's consent.

Asshole organ.

"Thank you, Mistress," I dare to whisper. I never know whether to thank her or not. Cane beats me either way, so it doesn't really matter.

"Did I say you could speak?" She screams at me, leering at me as though she's a judge and I've interrupted the court.

I cower in a ball, covering my head, muttering, "Sorry," over and over. She kicks me hard, and I can't breathe against the bone-shattering pain.

Escaping into my head is all I can do now. Like those dumb tech VR games I used to play. But I'm under Sergeant Pink Stiletto's control.

Dumb bitches and dogs. Fucking Dahlia Misery Catfish and her brigade of freaks.

Misery. The irony of her handle is not lost on me now. How can I miss it? I've got nothing else to do with my time but remember what I've done in the past. Because I don't have much of a present, and my future isn't looking too bright.

My nerves are fucked. She spooks me, jumping out and scaring me whenever she gets the chance. And her friends love looking upon me as some pathetic vermin. Or cat.

Ugh.

These stupid club of creepy Crow bitches raise their glasses and clink, then all glare at me.

"Congratulations Mistress. I hope you enjoy these special gifts today. And I'm looking forward to our Halloween dress up party soon!"

"Me too, I'm going as a masked man!" she says, and glares at me.

Fuck.

I cower as she goes to kick me, but stops short, holding the underside of her shoe for me.

"This is a fucking reward for you, Little Man. You have earned the right to lick now," she says.

My body works as though on auto. Cock throb, balls dead, hours of training and muscle memory making my limbs and head do their jobs. But I'm not here. I'm floating somewhere watching this bullshit from above.

My mind swirls with lean salmon, salmon jelly cat food, and squatting over a cat litter tray as she laughs at me and sprays me with Mistress Cane's piss. She turns up in her hoods and masks and different voices. Training me. Stretching my fucking asshole to please her and her weird cult of freaky goth bitches. Sneaking into my apartment at night. Taunting me. Teasing me as they laugh and howl.

I'm nothing but a wicked raggedy ass doll. Wrapped up in a rope bow.

Fucking wasabi bullshit.

She forces me to lick her fucking boot. It tastes disgusting, and I think back to the times I shoved an innocent woman's face into the dirt in a remote location.

The grit of the dirt from her shoe crunches between my teeth, as the tears slide into my cringing mouth. I want to scream.

All witch cunts of the highest order.

"I'm going to break you, you realise this don't you? You're lucky to be here, amongst these strong and powerful women. Maybe you're not as diabolical as I thought you were when I started investigating you. Now, let's get on with this neutering. I have a special blade here, especially for this, your personal sacrifices."

My nuts shrivel as I begin to hyperventilate. My vision tunnels into black, but I can still hear voices around me.

I am blind, and that only makes it worse. It's a fucking panic attack endless loop.

Fuck my life. She planned all this from the start.

Fucking Callsign Miss Misery bitchface from the zombie game. It's this bitch, Mistress Dahlia. Cane's right hand bitch, apprentice of sadism.

Holy shit, what have I got myself into here?

"You want to neuter me? What exactly does that mean?" I peep. But a stiletto to the ribs is my only reply.

[35]

MISS MISERY

IN MY BACK SHED, I'm hunched over my workbench, various bits and pieces of different animals lying about. I'm writing a poem to my dogs.

MISERY JOURNAL OF NIGHTMARISH
PROPORTIONS

ODE TO DOGS
You have nothing to worry about
Not a care in the world
No scavenging for food in garbage
Sometimes you jump the fence
Have a stormy night of worry and fright
But we pluck you out of neighbours' sheds
And off fences and out of laundry tubs

You wag your tails as we walk through
the door.
Even when you shit on the floor
There is a reason Dog is just God spelled
backwards.

I put my pen down and go back to stitching my human dolls together. I love using fresh body products.

A few random specimens of eyeballs and testicles line the rustic shelves around the room.

Previous rescue pets.

I like saving trophies from my adopted furry family.

It's always fun to remind them of why they're here.

Not so subtle reminders of the reason they ended up on my fucked-up radar.

This is a full-kill shelter. They don't get past me. No get out of jail free cards here.

Nope.

Just a 'slowly pay for your sins, or lose body parts at my discretion'.

[36]

MISTRESS CANE

I KICK him in the ass, as he crawls on all fours over the gravel, stark naked except for his kitten buttplug, ears and pink leather cat mask. I had it flown in from Germany, the craftsmanship is delicious, and it even has those sweet whiskers poking out from the snout. His delicious muscles ripple under the pink harness. His shiny cock cage keeps him in check, his balls a horror-filled stitched pancake. Cause he's still a fuckwit.

My long single tail whip cracks like thunder in the air, as it stings his ass perfectly. I roll it back toward me with a grin, and the scent of the leather gets my arousal surging. My nipples harden against my leather dress, and Callsign Shadow Fuckstain yelps like a goat. I watch with glee as a huge red welt forms instantly across his pale ass.

I don't give a shit what happens to his butt cheeks,

because he certainly never gave two shits about the revolving door of young women.

I hurry him along through public and luckily we don't raise too much attention, as I drag him toward the evening's location.

"Hurry up!" I growl my order at him at the same time I lodge my shoe right up his toned butt cheeks to tickle his fancy butt plug. "This is fun, isn't it kitty?"

"You'll never be able to show your stinky butt anywhere in cyberland, you silly kitten. You're a fucking idiot, guided by your impressive schlong, and you are a danger to young women.

And I'm the one they called in to clean up the mess. Kick you into shape. Test to see whether you're worthy of being rehabilitated for a while."

I stop and order Jamoa to piss on him, whilst I continue my crazy-woman rant at this pathetic rapist under my heel.

"You're nothing but a swamp rat. I'm your judge. If I find you unacceptable this evening, if you don't fulfill your purpose to my expectations, you'll have a pink bullet in your skull by sun up. If you please me, I'll hand you over to your new forever home. I think you know who it is. One of your best friends. Miss Misery. Otherwise known as my good friend, Mistress Dahlia. Anyway," I continue as Jamoa finishes his slash and slides his cock away. The cat is dripping in urine, and I start him up crawling again as I continue. "Unfortunately, we can't afford anaesthetic here, we're old school like that. From the bush. It's a rifle and a bullet, me old mate. And, you'll love this part. What's your favourite colour?"

He shakes his head, obviously he has no idea what I'm talking about.

"It's pink, cockhead. The weapon that will end your days will not be like your pussy video games. It will be bedazzled pink. So think about that one Kitten. I have to remind myself you're a cat sometimes. I see you in my mind as a pathetic dog that's been brought in for humping everything in town. Spreading disease, lies and destiny swaps. But someone called Justice on your scrawny ass. A vulnerable little bird. A swallow, if you will. And no, we'll never tell you who. I'm just your mirror. So you'd best be doing everything I say."

[37]

KITTEN POOPYGUTS THE THIRD

SHE GIGGLES as she calls me 'Fuck Nugget' on repeat.

As usual, this fucking Cane bitch has spent the entire day taunting me relentlessly, edging my dick and prostate until I'm about to spurt, then before I cum, she folds my cock in half, and squashes it back in my training cage.

Now, here I am, being dragged by my sparkly dog collar dingling with pink cat bells. MISTRESS CANE'S FOSTER ASHTRAY tag at the front. And I don't know what's worse, clenching the butt plug between my cheeks, or what will happen if I let it fall out.

I think back to the last time this thing fell out, when she rubbed my nose in my own shit. And I'm scared. She's been injecting me with all kinds of hormones after they neutered me. I can still get a hardon. I'm learning a lot about anatomy.

The hard way.

Fuck my actual real fucking life.

So I clench my sphincter tightly, once more, and sob inwardly as the gravel slices shreds out of my hands and knees. All that fucking money on my knee tats, bruh. All fucked now.

"Best behaviour now Shadow Kitten," she says. "The crows are watching you, ready to pluck out your eyes. You're on display, just like you love. The star of your own fucking show tonight. Sorry I couldn't get you a flak jacket, you understand, don't you pet?"

Another thunder crack in the air followed by a hot slash to my thighs.

"FML" I cry, wincing.

I'm used to pain now. I never got the masochist thing that all the brats are into. I could never imagine myself on the bottom, looking up to someone more powerful than me.

Because, before I met this tiny blonde shrew of a woman, I didn't think anyone was more powerful than me.

"I'm a cock head," I say out loud, projecting my voice perfectly.

"Yes you are!" she says, followed by a gaggle of laughter behind me.

She's dragged me to some exclusive party in some overly expensive wankers mansion. Not sure exactly where we are because the way we got here from my apartment, I was locked in the boot of the car.

So, I have no idea where I am, and she's quite proudly showing me off on our way to my death, or whatever the fuck is about to happen to me.

All I know is that I'm terrified for my life, because I can't risk going to jail. Not if that cat food blow job was any kind of example of what happens there.

"I fucked your Mum last night, Little Kitten. And she loved every second of it."

Her cool, sultry voice fills me with fear.

"You did not," I snarl back.

But yeah, I've got no idea if she's lying or not. She's an actual fucking psychopath.

This is the kind of bullshit she says to me all the time. She says I have "Mummy Issues," whatever they are.

She's been 'training me' for tonight, but the details have always been far too fucking vague for my liking.

Eventually we end up in a finely furnished room, with people standing around staring at me and pointing. Some giggle from behind their hands, masquerade masks of lace and leather, others in full latex hoods, all pointing and leering and laughing at me. The colour of my cheeks match the pink of the stupid mask she's padlocked on my head. A fucking cat, or mouse, or whatever stupid thing she's dressed me up as tonight.

I lock eyes with a young woman across the room, and I recognise her. The anger in her eyes tells me that I've fucked her in the past. And who knows how that ended. I am guessing I hurt more than her pride when I shoved her out the door shoeless.

I can't remember her or our interaction, and that's what scares me.

Who else is here? Hiding behind their Halloween masks, with their hidden agendas and revenge on their lips. Shit, if these bitches are dark romance girlies, who knows if they're packing knives in their thigh holsters, or even worse, pink fucking bedazzled hand weapons like fucking Mistress Cane.

A kick to my ass and I dip my nose to the floor.

"Look at me, pet," comes a familiar voice

I look up into the eyes of Dahlia, and I flinch. This bitch could have absolutely anything planned for me, and I am terrified that she has.

Little giggles from around the perimeter of the room, as dozens of people walk into the hall, all eyes watching me.

"Oh shit," I whisper under my breath as I watch these masked people pile into the room like a waterfall.

Fuck.

"Plow pose bitch. You're the ashtray for this room of smoking enthusiasts tonight. You are their performance art, nothing but a useful tool. Now, plow."

A harsh sting to my ass, and I sit down on the pain and roll onto my back, pushing my knees up either side of my head.

The giggles ramp up, and the scent of a variety of cigar, weed and cigarette smoke reaches my nose.

Fear swells inside me, as Dahlia giggles and pulls the cat plug from my ass, and inserts a speculum.

The pain rips from the inside, as she cranks it wide enough to fit a man's whole fist.

Tears roll down my cheeks silently, as I take this punishment and humiliation. Because there is no use fighting. It's either this or a shallow grave.

She leaves me there, coerced into bending into a goddamn pretzel, ass gaped wider than she's ever stretched it before this.

"This is what you've been training for over the last six months, babycakes. I wanted to use you, to stretch you open as wide and use you as a garbage can."

She cackles and her gaggle of bitches join in. But now I can hear men laughing too, all kinds of people are standing around watching me.

Fuck my life.

She leans down and hisses, "Don't you wish you had a safeword now, pet? Or, maybe the traffic light system? I bet you'd be calling red right about now, if you needed to."

I hear her giggling as she walks away, heels tap tap tap into the distance, and hot fat tears slide down both my temples.

The room fills with a thick layer of smoke, and I cough, blood pooling in my throbbing head, my limbs numb as time passes away, holding this crazy expert yoga for hours.

In groups and one by one, these faceless strangers step forward, ashing in my ass.

I need to shit, but it's going to be like black tar, and so embarrassing.

Their fucking cigars and blunts finding their powdery cinders up inside me. I'm perched on a tiny perspex stage, big enough only for me, like a fucking museum spectacle. An art gallery opening night with dramatic spotlights and the ever repetitive video evidence footage of me saying idiotic stupid shit like, *"Chicks don't need a safeword with me. If you need a safeword then you're not woman enough to handle my dick."*

How the fuck did I wind up here?

I bite back screams and howls that threaten to erupt. Tiny sparks of golden torture sting my ass tube as they flick their fire inside my colon.

The ever present metal cock cage presses into my face. My testicles are distant memories, as the empty sack gathers like a flat pancake, from the endless stitching she and her stupid friends have been up to on my fucking empty scrotum sack.

Fuck my life. I squeeze my wet eyes shut, and my soul leaves my body. I cannot be present here anymore.

I hear their laughter, like a fucking ghost. I watch this sinister cult of weirdos dressed in their finest velvet corsetry, feathers and fishnet, laughing and carrying on chatting and dancing to the throbbing classical music. Stepping up to my joke of a gaping asshole, and one even rests their cigar against my poor burned sphincter.

What I wouldn't give to be back in my apartment, with a callsign bratty sub on her way over to suck my dick.

I'm a living ashtray, used and abused as nothing but her fucked up artistic pursuits.

I'm her worm.

I'm starting to wonder whether this bullshit is actually better than death.

Maybe the Plague Doctor outside that house should have just shot me then and there.

Suddenly, my guts churn so badly, and I know, deep inside, I cannot stop this explosive diarrhea that is about to happen. Sweat drips out of every pore, and after hours of holding myself upside down, I risk sealing my grim fate.

"Mistress Dahlia, my goddess. Could I please be excused to use the restroom? I beg.

I hear the crack of a single tail whip. Every person stops speaking, and all eyes are on me.

"No! No, you may not be excused for the bathroom. Did you excuse all those women whose boundaries you crossed? Were they excused from decades of therapy because of you? The answer is no, cunt. You stay right where you are. This is why everyone is here, you dunce. Waiting for you to explode like a shit volcano, and now we're all going to laugh at you."

The searing pain in my guts eases as the flow of stinking black tar-like crap gurgles and spurts out my ass in a shooting explosion. Farts release in a symphony and merge into my pathetic wails, as the warm ooze settles into every orifice. The speculum keeps me gaped excessively. The taste in my mouth is her revenge. I spit my shit out, but it pools inside my sweaty kitten mask.

I feel a sting on my side as she kicks me over. Without care, she tears the speculum out, and I scream into the void. I feel the pink eye brewing already, as shit pools inside my eyeballs, and I can't see anything but darkness.

I can feel Dahlia's presence looming, and her fierce voice echoes off the walls of this sadistic torture palace.

"Shut up, sacrifice. Your plans backfired, baby. This is your future now."

[38]

KITTEN SCARED LITTLE MOMMY'S BOY THE HUNDREDTH

SHE DRAGS me up to the front of her goddamn house by a dumb unicorn dog collar, with a cruel, sadistic, spiky choke chain. Entirely unethical. The house is all freaky and black and exactly like a fucking Halloween scare house.

And the aesthetic has done its job, cause I'm fucking terrified as she drags me out of the van and throws me on the wet mud in her garden.

There is a grotesque man with his skin half ripped off his face, crouched under an apple tree, chewing on rotten fruit. He's mostly naked, chained by both arms to the tree on a very short chain, watching me from my place in the mud.

His eyes are terrifying. Just black orbs that look like they are a looking glass, straight into the bowels of hell.

A terrible chill runs through me, a look into the future. That he is me, in a few days from now. A few months, years, decades. It's all the same now. Every day the same as the last.

Fucking Halloween Bitches.

Oogy Boogy.

She shocks my collar, then stands above me. I look up, her heavy goth boots on either side of my face, and I look up this Misery Dahlia Bitch's sexy pussy as warm yellow liquid lands in a long, thick stream across my face.

Filling my mouth with disgusting piss, she laughs as the liquid splatters against her legs and into my eyes. She giggles as she jumps up and down, stepping on my ear, as she yanks me back up by the collar, and drags me past lines of kennels, each filled with different people, mostly men, cowering, eyes wide in fear as they watch her drag me on this fucking lead past them.

What the fuck is this?

She doesn't say a word as she drags me to my upcoming death.

[39]

MISTRESS DAHLIA

I LOCK the new cat smoke shadow fuckwit in his cage and slam the door, padlock clanging loudly. He's like a disoriented pigeon, pecking in the dust.

"You're mine, and you're totally fucked, aren't you, my tiny weeny little pathetic man baby?"

I ask Mr Adonis Kitten Narcissus, squashed into his new awful hell that I've meticulously constructed. "Is your mommy coming to get you soon from this super fun slumber party?"

I laugh, and he doesn't say a word.

I continue, shouting now, "No, your mommy isn't coming, I know, cause I just fucked her. You're a cock head. It was a great decision to get you neutered. That Goddess Paradox is one woman to admire. Her steady hand, her sadistic mind. We make a great slicey-dicey team, don't cha think?"

I lower my voice to a whisper as he attempts to dissociate from this fresh hell I've conceived. I rattle his cage and his biggest fears."Now, I am your fucking master, bitch, and I have ensured that no more little Smoke Shadow Kitten Worm babies will be crawling around in wombs. Look at your specimen in my jar."

His eyes unwillingly look at the jar containing two floating testicles, and he winces, looking away again. I laugh.

He remains mute as I say, "No more women being taken advantage of by your wimpy widdle pee pee. You're fucked, aren't you?"

He risks replying this time, "Yes Mistress. I'm royally fucked. I'm your worm, and you are ready to tear me in half and laugh as you do it."

I say, "Don't you worry about that. I have access to some archaic torture methods; drawing and quartering your ass wouldn't be beyond my means. I hate your fucking guts, always have, even when I was lying in this very bed, getting myself off over your jacobs piercings and dick tattoo. How are they going by the way? Those piercings getting stuck in your cock cage? That would be a shame, wouldn't it? You made me cringe and cum at the same time, and for that, I'll never let you go again. And I'm only going to add to your dick and ballsack jewellery. Cause you're mine. Only mine. Till death do us part. And as it happens, you're exactly the kind of toy my friends love to shit stir. And they have plenty of ideas.

Just like how I modified your testicles, but it's only going to get worse, Kitten."

In abject terror Kitten glares at the jar containing his formaldehyde suspended manhood. I've added an uplight for full Halloween effect. Styled it off a mad scientist. He gets the vibe. He doesn't like it much.

"Hey, every fucking day is Halloween around here bitches."

I giggle as I kick his cage again for dramatic effect and switch on some of the diabolical audio recording's I've saved of him ranting about women or any minority he could think of. He turns his head away.

I can tell he wants to shout obscenities at me, but Mistress Cane has trained that kind of bullshit out of him. I've adopted a house trained pet, and he loves his lavender cat litter and salmon puree the best. And his hamster's drink bottle with the pipe certainly gets a good deep throat every day.

I think back to all those times he treated me like dirt late at night; the relentless bullying reduced me to tears, not because of what he said, but because of triggers to my past violent relationship. To those times when I was taken advantage of by any man in my vicinity.

Raised to be groomed for men to put their filthy hands wherever they please, and even if they're caught by the cops, they end up with no punishment. Nothing. He hid behind new usernames, profile pictures, and voice-pitching tech. He thought I was and would forever be a stranger to him. I was just a "psycho" chick because I refused to meet him in a secluded location. Or in his apartment. I'm so glad that Cane has balls of steel.

But no. This shithead deserves everything that is unfolding.

I say in a sexy voice, "You're so fucking fucked, it's not funny."

He winces as I cross my room to the craft section and grab the poster and packet of Blu-Tac.

It's been two weeks since the Smokers Lounge party, and I smile at the memory of him bent in half like a taco, bearing the brunt of a room full of smoking fetishists, all coming for the spectacle and chance to degrade a rapist.

I press my thumbs into the blue tack, sticking his rules. I've printed it in an extra-large font, just in case this dunce can't read. Sometimes I'm not sure about him at all, especially whether he has an education past primary school.

He certainly got himself a little education in rape and cyber stalking, blackmail, so, maybe these rules will help. Give him another chance. I always feel sorry for these beasts who refuse to learn a lesson. Who everyone wants to kill with no remorse.

No matter, it's all worth it to teach this silly poopyface a lesson. And if he fucks up, I'll just have to carve him up and feed him to the pigs in my barn. They eat anything, those fuckers.

From henceforth, you shall be known as "Kitten Kevin Poopityface the Nineteenth."

I have provided you with a pen and a notebook. You can start your lines simply by writing your name. Fill this book by tomorrow night. Oh, and welcome to your new forever home, where I'll make sure you're uncomfortable, twenty-four hours a day. You sticky, pathetic twat. Hope you like your cellmates. They should have lots of stories to share.

[40]

KITTEN KEVIN STINKYFEET I'M FUCKED

THE ROOM IS DARK, only the chilling red lights of her high tech surveillance glows. Her sound proofing is even better than mine is — was — in my self made porn studio.

I wonder what happened to that place. I fucking loved that bed with the stocks.

The door opens and a pin point of light sweeps through the shadows. The outline of a cloaked figure enters, and the light blinds me as the person finds their target in the night.

Me.

"Oh, there you are scumbag. Remember me? No? Well, I definitely remember you, three years ago, Halloween. The way you drugged me, that night is seared into my mind for other reasons. Other things you did and said to me. Remember?" I shake my head. "And so, here I am, simply to get my eye, for an eye."

"Oh fuck," I say.

She moves quickly, jolting my electric dog collar. She opens the cage and grabs my head, snapping my neck back painfully.

She produces a switchblade from her cleavage, and without warning, the shiny tip of the blade comes for me, stabbing in around my eyeball, and popping it out. I scream and flail, but it's all too late. My eye is out, and I hear the ripping and tearing of my viscera, as she yoinks it out and shoves me back inside the cage. My hands fly up to cover my eyes, but it's too late. She's standing there with my eyeball dripping blood down her arm, and above my howls all I can hear is her snickering, as she turns around and heads back for the illuminated doorframe.

She says, "You're nothing but a circus sideshow freak. You don't agree with consent, and so here we are. This is called karma, babyshadow. Oh, I had a lot of fun at the Halloween Smoke Lounge Ball. I dressed up as a sexy as fuck goth vampire queen, fangs and all, and I spat whiskey in your gaping asshole after I ashed in it with my Queenly cigar. Fuck you baby, you're nothing but a goddamn ashtray."

She walks out, slams the door, and leaves me crying

with a searing migraine, bleeding out of my eye socket, and wanting to die.

[41]

KITTEN I HAVE NO NAME

THE SOLID STEEL bars loom in on me as my panic attack skyrockets. Misery Dahlia has done everything to make sure I'm as humiliated as possible.

I fear not only her human powers of persuasion but also the supernatural. Those women are involved in some strange blood rituals. Constantly sticking IVs in me, injecting mystery substances. Drawing my blood. Drinking it in front of me.

They creep me the fuck out. And they appear out of nowhere.

My gut tightens at the thought of what they are doing to me. And what will happen tomorrow? In an hour. In a second.

I cringe at my behaviour in the past. Maybe, at some point, I could have prevented this.

If I hadn't gone to that party.

If I hadn't hooked up with Pepper.

If I hadn't raped those girls.

This awful cage is now my forever home. The tiny Hello Kitty baby blanket she has given me is too small to cover my chest. But that's okay, because I can't stretch out to my full height of six feet four anyway. I'll never be happy or comfortable. I'm always cold and numb, watching her piled under her mountains of fresh and warm blankets.

The Mistress Bitch Brigade has made certain that I'm as miserable as possible.

My legs shake and twitch and burn with cramps, and I stare in horror as Callsign Miss Misery bitch opens her bedroom door, and switches on the bright overhead light with no warning.

My eye burns. She knows I am scared of overhead lights now, and my dick goes from flaccid to pushing painfully against the chrome cage, strangling my cock. My balls, gone. My eye, gone.

A mangy-looking naked slag is crawling through the door, head hung low. Misery Bitch slides open a large cupboard door to reveal a row of bird cages. They would be a decent size for a pair of finches, but I know what's about to happen.

And the woman on the floor looks up in horror as Misery Bitch thwacks her across the ass with a pink riding crop.

"Everyone, this is Ratty Stinkyface Dutch-Oveness the First. Get in now, you fucking cunt," she says to the woman. "Everyone, rat-faced-cunt is your new kennel fresh hell friend. She was one of your little groupies, fuckface shadow kitten. Stirred up reams of bullshit that I'm sure Interpol cyber crime unit would be happy to deal with. Ratty bitch has bullied people into suicide, and that is why she has had to be re-homed. She cannot live without her phone."

Misery Dahlia turns to the new woman and says, "I think six months in this cage is a place to start with you bitch. You've been having fun down the well, haven't you?" I watch as Misery boots Ratty with the force of an MMA master, and I cringe, remembering the way her kick felt on my balls.

When I had them. I cringe at my future.

No more girls gargling my balls in their 'no gag reflex' throats. Silent tears fall for the memory of my balls.

When they weren't floating in that fucking god-awful lava lamp full of my misery.

Fucking Miss Misery. At least she got one thing right. Catfished me with a sexy goth badass name.

I stare dumbfounded as this rank bitch scurries awkwardly into the tiny cage. Now I see the black and blue bruises covering her rib cage, and again I wince, remembering the night fucking Mistress Cane barged into my life and turned my life into a living nightmare.

My hearing fades back in, and I listen in like a fly on the wall. She's speaking directly to the rat-faced bitch currently in her scope and focus of her current rant.

"You're a war pig. You and all your stupid toxic little gang of mean girls. The crows warned you, silly billy. You sent out your skanky ass minions to do your dirty work. You turned into a vapid ghost and you lured Kitten's young women into dark situations. We have your browser history, little rat. We have your hard drives and extracted farm of burner phones, just like that cockhead over there, with a cat plug up his ass and missing his manhood."

I shudder as she continues. "Ratty McFuckface, you're nothing but a discord pimp. Your diabolical magic has led you to me, didn't it baby cakes? Whatever your current handle online is, it doesn't matter cause you're gone.

I've Control Alt Deleted your feral little hive."

A shudder runs down my spine as everyone is silent.

Ugh.

A drop in temperature has me shuddering, as Mistress Dahlia Miseryguts levels her icy gaze at me.

She points at me. "No more trolling the internet."

She points to the weird Ferret Man with the long brown beard with a rainbow bow. His beer gut and tiny prick on display. I don't look at him if I can help it. She crouches over his cage, taunting him, rattling the metal.

"No more raping."

"What the fuck?" I whisper under my breath.

Misery points to Ratty.

"No more lying and raising witch hunts in cyber towns. No more trafficking women without frontal lobes into the insidious trades. You're all a little piece of the evil that spreads freely through the corrupt elite. You all end with me. Aren't you so lucky to be here with me? Hey, you can listen as I play the zombie game. You're gonna love that, aren't you, Callsign Smoke Shadow Daddy. Or should I call you Kitten? Or maybe, I'll come up with another new name for you, Kitten Kevin the Twenty-Fifth. Cause, you know, there is nothing special about you, Shadow Daddy."

And Misery Dahlia isn't fussy about gender when it comes to vengeance.

Somehow, Ratty's ended up on the crow coven's shit list as well as every other creepy fucking dude here.

I almost feel a pang of sympathy, but I cough it away. I need to vomit, but nausea is my everyday life now. I'm long past detoxing. I'm dying for a fucking cone. Or a painkiller. That does not exist here.

No.

I get ferret and cat food, and water with fucking dick pills in them.

So she can edge me with her sultry voice. Fuckery uno reverse karma bullshit. But they always seem to know everything about us.

Cane knew my complete history before she ever kicked my front door in and zapped me down six pegs in one fell swoop.

Bitches, the lot of them. Outsmarted me at every fucking turn. And the dumb thing is that they warned me.

A hot tear dribbles down my cheek pathetically as I watch the dumb woman climb into the tiny cage, like a contortionist. She folds in on herself; she cannot stretch her legs out either. She's obviously going to be here for the long haul.

Just like me.

And suddenly it dawns on me. Mistress Dahlia Misery Bitch is a spider, somehow hiding under a curled leaf in a bush, just waiting for the wrong person to get caught in her web of surveillance.

I knew better than to fall for dark romance girlies. But those e-girl STEM nerdy bitches are smart. A shitload smarter than I could ever pretend to be.

Fucking crow club. They should rebrand as the fucking Murder of Catfish.

But here I am, pathetic as ever.

And they are watching. Spying. Hacking into my hard drives and extracting all the evidence that I was holding against women. And they fucked me in the ass, literally.

Misery locks the cage and shuts the door, popping the key on the hook with mine. The new captive, Rat, is alone in the dark. Squashed. Confined. My claustrophobia wraps its awful claws around me, and I look at my cage bars again.

"I'm watching you, babycakes," comes the crackled voice over the hidden speakers. "I'm always watching you, cause I'm a voyeur bitch. And you won't see me coming for you in the night. Watch your dick, it might end up in a glass jar, next to your crown jewels."

[42]

KITTEN ASSHOLE THE STRETCHIEST STARFISH THE
TENTH

"WHAT'S YOUR NAME?" she asks, her voice yet again different.

Her eyes staring at me with the kind of evil I've never seen before.

I glance behind her to my keychain which she proudly hangs on the wall as my reminder of how far I've come in the last year.

"My name is KITTEN ASSHOLE THE STRETCHIEST COUNT THE TENTH, Mistress." I shout my newest stupid name as loudly as I can. Projecting my voice so clearly with my well rehearsed fry.

The bitches love the fry.

"That's right. And who owns you?"

"You do, Mistress. I belong to Mistress Dahlia."

I watch her, from my corner in her huge bedroom — THE STINKY RESCUE PET CORNER — as she likes to call it. She also has the 'stables' out the back full of 'horses and goats', and some weird creatures she keeps in the basement. But I'm rarely let out of this room so I don't know exactly what is downstairs, which creeps me the fuck out. Because she rescued and rehabilitated me, but unfortunately, even though lovingly trained by the infamous Mistress Cane I'm not fit for the public.

"What are you pet?" she asks.

I swallow the lump in my throat, and groan as the need to take yet another black shit overtakes me. I recite the lines I have written over ten thousand times already.

I clear my throat and say loudly and clearly, projecting my voice to the best of my ability. Using my sexiest fry, I say,

"I am not fit to be returned to polite society. I must remain forever chained where I can't hurt anyone. In the care of my loving Mistress. I am cared for, and loved."

No tears fall anymore, not since I accepted my fate. Could have been worse. She could very well let one of those ex-military fuckers shoot me, but I'm alive. Yes, I spend all my days and nights, squatting over my lavender scented cat litter tray, and sleep squashed into my tiny dog cage, where I can't even stretch out all the way.

"Purr for me baby," she says, tickling me under the chin as she licks a pink lollipop.

I purr for her, the noise that I know soothes her in the night.

"Good boy. Now baby pickle pants, I'm going to put you in your frilly pyjamas now, your favourite onesie with the zip up the front. I'm going to take selfies and put them on the internet. Show your victims what you're up to these days. They love getting their updates. They cackle at your pathetic excuse for a life now, without your tough guy masks and microphone bullshit. Now, when I let you out of this cage, you have to be a good boy? You know how to be a good boy now, don't you? Goddess Cane has taught you so well, hasn't she? She broke you in for my needs. She gave me a beautiful gift, in you. She broke you, bucking bronco. Now I've saddled you, and I'm about to ride you across the western apocalyptic landscape, and fuck you into oblivion. And that's if you're lucky."

"Yes, Mistress," I say. "I'll be sleeping in the dog house with the strays."

"That's right. Now come here and let me get you dressed."

I do as she says, allowing her to dress me up like some kind of twisted Ken doll. Raising my arms as she dresses me in a stupid onesie and brushes my hair. Taking pictures and uploading them to the internet. I'm a joke.

She told me that my fans stopped looking for me after a few weeks, and now I'm just faded into history, along with all the other masked book boyfriend wannabes.

And my Mistress invites the other crow members over to play stabby slicey games with their fucking hunting blades.

I know I'm lucky to be alive. During those god-awful, endless nights that blended into one chained starfish in my bed. Chained in my lambswool manacles I designed and installed to keep sexy, thick-thighed, badass goth kittens spread and open for my cock.

This insane gaggle of psychotic bitches loves taunting me, popping around with their shiny keys, letting themselves in at any hour of the day or night. It's their goddamn hobby; they collect us like circus animals for their little private freak show. They shove sounding rods up my dick while they giggle and sip champagne.

Or reminding me every second of the goddamn day and night that they've buried creepy men for less than what I've done.

I drag my hands and knees across the floor as I crawl out of my solid steel dog cage. Bending to lap fresh water from the cat fountain, I sip back the cool liquid. The hamster water bottle is always in my cage.

With its stupid tiny ball bearing I have to lick lick lick like a fucking ferret.

Ugh,

I hate her.

Treating me like a gerbil.

Oh shit.

Not a fucking gerbil.

Can she hear my thoughts.

Please don't shove a gerbil up my ass.

Oh fuck, she'd totally do that too.

STOP THINKING ABOUT GERBILS FUCK HEAD.

She's been experimenting with my tongue with her sinister surgical tools and body mod practice. I long to drink an extra large can of peach flavoured energy drink in one long glug.

I drag my rattling ankle chain, connected to the sturdy surgical steel cuff around my right ankle, and it allows me enough extension to lay on the oversized dog bed in the corner to sleep on. It's a pink fluffy blanket, with a My Little Pony cushion. I lay my head on the rainbow pillow and sigh.

I glance across at the other fully grown man, cowering with a variety of old and new scars across his face. The latest one is a bright red line that goes from his receding hairline, right across his brow and down the side of his cheek.

Miss Misery, Mistress Dahlia, or whatever her real fucking name is.

She calls the other man "Noodle McTacoCunt" or something. He hasn't told me his real name.

Miss Misery, Mistress Dahlia, whatever her real name is, even started calling ME Baldy McButtplug. She terrifies me, making me forever stay in a solid metal cock cage and keeping a light-up buttplug in my ass at all times.

"Fucking bitch," I whisper under my breath.

I've whispered to him before, when she's been out at work, even though she keeps tabs on us 24/7. I'm taking a risk by whispering with her in the room, but she's wearing her soundproof headphones, keeping tabs on the next rapist out there who will end up just like me and old mate here with me.

I glance up at the red lights dotted around the room. Her surveillance cameras, always watching us. This ferret-bearded man hates her as much as I do. He says he used to rape girls who went on early morning jogs through the park. She tasered him and threw him in a white van.

And this is the end of the story. At least we're not six feet under.

[43]

KITTEN ROYAL KITTEH POOPYFACE

I PRACTISE my beatboxing in my head, as I look across the room to another man in the opposite corner of the room. He whimpers quietly, but bitchface ignores him just like she ignores me. He's a small guy, scrawny and pathetic. Completely bald, with prison tattoos covering every inch of his flesh. She calls him Fluff. Or Fluffy McFloofenhousen. I can't keep up with her stupid names, she seems to have a new one for us every day. But from what I've gathered, this decrepit Fluff bloke is missing both his eyes.

Like totally, no eyes, no patch. Nothing, just two deep hollows in his skull with a thin layer of white skin. Apparently he lost both eyes in a prison stay. Seems he was lucky to walk out of the razorwire fence alive, from the sounds of things, this creep has fiddled and diddled little kiddies, and that's why then these dumb fucking dominatrix network of cyber bitches swooped him up at first chance. Murmurs from my cell mates in chains here, is that this crime ring of angry bitches set to work continuing the good slasher and shanking work from the inmates behind bars. These crazy psycho whores keep carving him up, over and over, and keeping him alive and his pain level and misery through the roof. They never let them heal properly, keep them alive and degraded, rather than put the world out of its misery. These miserable cunts have taken their role of Masked Vengeance Seekers.

As though reading my thoughts, she meets my gaze and says, An eye for an eye, cockhead. Death is too good for the lot of you," she says from her place on her pillow fortress. She's like the fucking princess and the pea in her layers of lace and frills.

[44]

RATTY SERVERBITCH

THIS PLACE IS TERRIFYING.

Fucking Miss Misery dumped me here eons ago, and I've been alone since.

I shudder as the heavy metal grate pulls back scraping across the concrete, and she calls down to me.

"Ratty! Oh Ratty McStinkyface! How are you, my little feral rodent? Are you hungry? How are you coping without your phone? How do you spend your days without the ability to cyber bully your victims?"

A twinge of guilt for my past actions. Some victims felt more romantic than others. Sometimes, I thought they loved me. She's right. I've got nothing to do with my time anymore, but pluck the bugs from where they nest, buried beneath my flesh. Burrowing toward my heart.

She begins to sing, slurring every word.

"Ring around a Rosie ..... a pocketful of ...... dead rats!'

She cackles again, smoking her joint.

The parasites she feeds me are gnawing me from within.

She's got me down a well now, it's been weeks or months. Halloween, as she always says. I think I'm out the back of her property but I can't know for sure. I could be anywhere. The drugs she's shoved down my throat have turned this nightmare into psychological torture. She pops in to check on me every few days. Every now and then she comes to visit me, drunk and loud. She'll sit up at the top of the well, throwing shit down at me, screaming stories and bullshit about some chick she used to love.

She rambles for hours, swigging whiskey and pissing on me from above.

I'm scratching myself raw, my flesh hanging off in chunks. Constantly picking nits out of my hair, and bugs out of my ears. She infiltrates my dreams, all versions of her I've ever met. She's chasing me through the streets and tunnels, blood dripping. I'm her prey.

I hate her so much.

A kilo of cheese knocks off my head and lands on the stone with a thud. In the dim light, I see the green mold covering the cheese.

"That's your dinner for the next week, so make sure to ration."

This is worse than any detox or rehab. I never knew horror like this could exist until I slid into Miss Misery's fucking DMs. Worst fucking decision of my life.

I inhale a long breath, and scream as loud as I can, "Fucking freak!" Before screaming the most blood curdling scream I can in the hopes that some random hiker is walking by. But it's no use. She's buried me good and proper, somewhere that time has forgotten.

After my hearing returns, she flicks her cigarette butt at me from above, and begins another of her neverending fucking monologues about fuck knows what. Half the time I can't tell if any of it is real, but I'm starting to put the pieces together. I'm pretty sure she killed her ex.

I settle back into my cardboard box home, and listen to her rant.

"My victims screamed in their last moments. Tasted the salty ocean mixed with clotted semen as you swallow through your pearl and golden necklaces! I jerked that out of them before I slaughtered them in my back shed abattoir. Oh, Ratty. They're all hanging up like the animals they are. Their cocks and balls and tongues dehydrated and saved for later. You would know about that though, wouldn't you little shit? Just like cattle, or a rat. You're nothing but a sewer rat you know. And I've got some fun adventures through the underground tunnels. Don't worry, you'll have fun. You'll be just another one of my special victims. My special bed-and-breakfast rescue of the insidious, and you're just culinary torture for the insects dietery needs. Those little insects are miracles, aren't they? Especially the roaches, oh, they will recycle your putrid flesh into something much more positive. Perhaps this is where you belong after all, little cunt.

You've got it good! I milked some of my other victims' cocks and in their moment of climactic release, I collected their seed into a jar and labeled it with a purple ribbon. I sold it, haha.

Lobster bisque with ravioli with human fluids anyone? Fresh from the ocean this morning! Come and get it!"

Her maniacal words filter from reality into my dreams, and I drift away into another cyber nightmare fresh hell, as the rodents scurry across my cold body, and the lice chew their way across my scalp. I even scratch in my sleep.

This is a fresh kind of hell, and Callsign Miss Misery is the newest face of Satan.

Searing strobes of lights flash in my mind, and laughter from above. When my vision and consciousness seep back, I can see red flashing lights.

Laughter stops, and she says, "Thanks for the content. Your victims enjoy logging in every day to watch your stupid little show. You were always so great at spouting nonsense online, and now they're giggling from behind their screens, laughing at your pathetic outcome. You're a rat. See you next time!"

I swallow, my mouth dry. I lean over and lick some mossy sludgy water from the cave wall and close my eyes against the agony of life.

Her voice from a distance rings out, "You were warned, two years ago. The crows are always watching your ass."

[45]

MISTRESS CANE

I GRAB Hemschris by his cock, jerk it toward my Pumpkin Spiced Frapuccino, and insert it into the freezing slush.

He gasps, his enormous balls tightening at the temperature assault, but remains still like the filthy dog he is.

"Not a drop spilled, good boy," I say, and a smile spreads across his face. "Here, take this."

He grips the plastic cup, holding it around his cock as his dumb grin gets wider.

"Now, go and fuck Jamoa, and make it extra messy for your Goddess, won't you?"

He does as I asked, skipping away to find his pack mate, as I grin and press start on my phone. As I watch the seconds count by I prop it up against a pot plant to record it for later purposes. I love watching my pups hump each other, covered in Halloween cheer.

I lounge back in the sun chair and pop two kernels of salted caramel popcorn into my mouth, crunching. My saliva pools as I watch Hemschris fucking the frappe cup, and then aims it toward my Jamoa's slutty asshole.

My favourite good boy.

Yes, I think Jamoa is my favourite. I'll admit that publicly, I don't care what anyone thinks. I might even ask him to sleep in my bed one of these nights. And not in the plush purple furry cage nest under my bed where he dozes most nights.

Protecting me as he should.

We're sitting in the backyard. I'm in my sundress, a leather holster around my thigh, and my pupcakes are watching me from where they're fucking and rolling around and groaning on the lawn.

I giggle as I watch Hemschris top Jamoa's tall frame with ease,

sip my cocktail and glance across at Dahlia, who is reclining on her sun lounge. She smiles at me.

She's a voyeur too.

[46]

KITTEN COCKHEAD

"You're a cockhead," she says, before going back to sip her red iced tea with a fucking mint sprig on top.

"I hate you," I say. My voice is weak and thin.

I roll over and poke out my hideously stitched tongue and sadly lick my hamster water ball. She's propped in her bed as usual, bullying me, taunting me.

And now she growls, "That's awesome, cause I hate you too. I'm always on your six, watching you, cause you're a fucking idiot. Shut up and go to sleep, or I'll shoot you in the dick."

[47]

MISTRESS DAHLIA

"WHAT ARE YOU LOOKING AT, my little Kitten Ashtray butt? I'm the belle of this brawl, and you're the dunce." I ask my three-legged human cat. He glares at me with raging hatred because he loves it when I give him a new name every five minutes and a new tag and bells on his pink zappy electric jolt collar every morning.

"Silly billy Poopy face," I say with glee, as I kick my heel up under his guts. Massaging one of his lesser organs.

He loves my hilarious, gallows sense of humour.

He gets the jokes. He understands the irony.

Maybe.

Or maybe the girls are right, and he will never learn his stupid lesson. No matter. I'm not threatened by a weak little dick like him. I'll use him until I have no use for him anymore. And if he gets into dogfights with the assholes living in my barn, then, good luck to him.

May the best asshole win. I don't give two shits.

Princess Kitten Lubed-Starfish the Sixty-Ninth with that dumb expression in his pretty blue eyes.

He is handsome, especially now that his leg is gone. He still does everything I ask. He takes care of me, his goddess, as he should.

He's so dumb. He chanced a look up at my glorious figure perched atop his firm peach of an ass.

I look around at all my sexy friends, their wigs, hair tucked up under caps, hiking clothes and bottles all held by our various dogs and pack mules. I've even brought one of my jackasses along for the outing to the lighthouse lookout here today. He's laden down on all sides with my cold, packed lunch.

These animals are kept busy with various tasks to keep the crows happy in their day-to-day lives.

Always respectful.

Always obeying our commands.

Always dealing with the next absurd idea I come up with for extreme body modifications. I think back to when I inserted some metal horns into his dumb head. He's lucky I haven't tattooed something across his forehead yet.

And that's only because I haven't decided what to write. I could go so many ways with this one.

"Ooh, you're nasty, aren't you, little Kitten? You showed your true hand, and the crows recorded every second of it." I say this low, my voice a warning growl.

But my friends hear. They hear everything.

The coven turns to watch me, faces alight with mischief, all as sadistic as each other.

We turn to Mistress Cane for her leadership once more. She's grinning from her seat atop the impromptu bronze human throne she's reclining upon. The distant ocean, a glistening backdrop to her enchanting ways.

"This is so fun, isn't it?" she asks the awestruck crowd.

She's turning her face to the sunshine's warmth and exhales slowly. "I've really needed a weekend away with my gorgeous pack. To be in the woods, hunting, is always such a pleasure with my collective."

"I'll say. I've enjoyed getting this aggressive cockhead out for some social interaction. You've trained him exceptionally well, Mistress Cane, if I may be so bold. I strive to one day be as cool as you," I say. Framing that as a joke, but I meant every word.

The human dogs under Cane's firm thighs are mute, with their cute puppy butt plugs hanging out of their bare asses, and their thick leather puppy masks and thick collars firmly in place. They will break her fall in any circumstance.

She loves to torment these bronzed gods with glistening smiles a mile wide. She fucks with their heads relentlessly, but they keep coming back for more. Their nefarious streams of income aren't her concern; all that matters is that her needs are taken care of at all times.

And as I've witnessed these men literally jump in front of bullets for her, whatever this odd little thing that she's got going on with them, it works.

They're all happy, in their fucked-up way.

Just as I am content with my 6'4" Kitten under my perky rear.

I look down at him and scratch him behind the ear. He scowls at me, absolutely furious that I turned his stupid predator into such a pleasant and agreeable pet.

This is one of the rarest days I let him out of his STINKY SHITPET CORNER.

I bring him out occasionally, humiliate him, and show everyone his latest war wounds. He has long been missing an eye and two testicles, both of which he sees every day, under the spotlight, like some fucked up lava lamp; he has to stare at his body parts. No hope for the future.

And he hates me. Just the way it should be. Just the way he always has from the very start. His position underneath me is exactly where he belongs and shall remain.

I lean down and say to him, "Kitten. Unfortunately, because of your behaviour," I whisper to him. "You will never have another owner. It's either me, or a shallow grave, just like Tom over there." I nod toward the bushland we just came from.

Tonight I'm going to stuff my foam ear plugs in and psyops torture him with RESPECT song.

It's one of my favourites, and I know he loves it too.

"Checkmate, Kitten. You were warned, back when you were the alpha hero, and now look where we are. Out here in nature, and you're nothing but my gaping trashcan with an annoyingly arousing voice. Now, pick me up, and carry me back to the car. My legs are sore."

[48]

"Happy Halloween, babycakes. How are you finding your dwellings? You're so sweet. But no one is coming for you, pathetic pieces of shit. You're all a pack of discord-inducing whores. But not anymore. This is as good as it's going to get for the lot of you. And your days left on earth are up to me. Your forever owner, the one who loves her squishmallows, bubble pumpkin spice tea latte bullshit drinks, and fluffy sox. I can put you all down on a whim.Now shut the fuck up, every last one of you. Not a complaint, not a fucking fart. Shut up. Vermin, the lot of you. You too my little overflowing cupboard of rats in there. All you bitches festering away in my little tiny bird cages. Little rat rat ratties squashed in the dark and dusty cupboard. Where you all belong. How are you going to suck Callsign Smoke Shadow Daddy's balls if he's stuck in my stinky pet corner? Oh that's right. He ain't got no balls, cause he ignored the warning of the crows. Silly boy. Silly girls. I hate you all."

She switches off the lights and puts her annoying cheery positive affirmations loud on the surround sound stereo. The affirmations merge and mashup with the nightmare inducing songs of strong women's anthems. My intense horror filled dreamloop nightmares of my body parts being removed, merged into my memories and neverending captive waking hours. They never let me sleep. Never a full sleep cycle, and so my deprivation has turned into shadows on the walls, and paranoia so strong I think I'm insane.

My throbbing pink pierced and tatted masked manhood facade of the past is a faint and distant memory. How long has it been since Cane appeared in my apartment? I'll never know. These bitches say it's Halloween every single day. So I'll never know the date. Every day is Groundhog Day around here. And I'm the fucking groundhog.

I thought she was nothing but an e-girl whore, and now. Here we are.

She plays these stupid mental health sleep music all damn night, on repeat, but she doesn't listen to it. No, it's for our feral ears only. She stuffs foam earplugs in her own ears so she hears nothing but her sweet dreams.

She sleeps soundly with me in the stinky pet corner. She spied me online and had to have me for herself.

Fuck my life.

I don't deserve this. I'm Callsign Smoke Shadow Daddy god damn it. All my fans creamed over my vocal skills, I have to remind myself. I wonder if they're thinking about me since my last appearance as a masked porn star. With tears now streaking my cheeks, and my giant tatted pierced cock and flat stitched drilled and punctured nuts stuffed into this cage. My leg is a stump, missing an eye, teeth, shit inserted under my flesh, my testes swimming in a jar I look at every day.

Ratty coughs from the cupboard of stinky skanks, or whatever the closet is called today.

I hate all those dumb emo bitches. My minions and whore groupies. The people who tell me they love me, and support me, then turn their fucking back when I can't get them into Hollywood, or porn, or whatever.

[49]

MISERY DAHLIA THE FIRST

I HARNESS UP THE RATTY, the Kitten, and the OG Fluff, and yank them out the back door by their choker chains, on their naked hands and knees. My rain boots splash in the puddles, as we go for a lovely walk around the bushland on my property.

Well, the pets are crawling on their hands and knees if they have them. Most of them are missing multiple body parts, which have already been used in my back shed house of horrors.

Ratty's guts are on display now, poor thing; she doesn't have much time left on this earth, so I've brought her out for her final stroll in nature. Let her feel the wind on her face, as her tears stream down her cheeks. I'll take some photos of her later, as a poignant warning to the nefarious bitches watching her demise.

No more hooglly googly destiny swaps, voodoo hoodoo bullshit can change the outcome of their fate.

"No more tea to be sipped in your servers, by you dumb bitches. You're all fucked, aren't you? Evil, every last one."

"Yes, Mistress. We are royally fucked," they say in unison. Their zombie eyes glazed and dissociated.

"You're all rejected. You're blocked by the ancestors. This shit is stopping with the Crows."

I stare down at Ratty, covered in maggots, and the other pets stare at her in disgust and revolt.

She's the worst of the lot of them.

"I call your bullshit. Your shit is going down."

[50]

MISERY JOURNAL OF NIGHTMARISH PROPORTIONS

You are the keeper of your own
records.
Guardians of the wilderness
With twigs in their hair and wild eyes
The stones vibrate
We are but bones under the earth
Rivers of colours, a riot of
imagination.
Buried for too long in the womb of
the mother but rising again
The power is in the symbols
A sacred ceremony
Cross-quarter fires
Every event that's ever unfolded
Now unfolds in your lap

It lays its head down and breathes
you in
      Nestles between your thighs
      Drinks in the youness of you, that only
you can provide.
      And the parties on the Islands,
bonfires and wine and night swimming
under the Milky Way.
      Spiced treats and spicier nights.
      Hot bodies and fragrant oils
      Resins in another time, another era
only available to us in our nightly dreams
      When we step through the doorway of
consciousness.
      I was angry. Sad. Consumed with
grief.
      The human gelatin simmered the
delectable jam on top of it. Nice and
firm, the fruit chunks held their shape.
      I enjoyed preserving, fermenting, and
other scientific methods used to prolong
the lives of my human sacrifices.
      The scent of bleach lingered long
after I wiped my benches clean. Perhaps
I have OCD.

I sprinkled my dehydrated human-heart powder, blended with the smoked paprika and cumin mix. Side serving of beans and asparagus. A light vinaigrette.

Oysters done in the smoker—under my crush Rhiandra's watchful gaze—with garlic, chilli, and pepper berry. Someone inserted human semen into the plump sea creatures with a syringe. Extra gooey textures, as my esteemed patrons will swallow into their gullets. One lovely, aphrodisiac swallow.

[51]

RATTY BITCHFACE

I TWIST and turn my head, but all I can see is the sprawling abyss of my mind. Floating and crumbling in some crazy stratosphere.

In and out of tunnels, coloured lights whizzing past, my body parts removed, lucid recurring nightmares about being eaten from the inside out by parasites. Nightmares about the months I spent down that fucking well, in that network of tunnels that will forever haunt my dreams until the day I die.

Which, let's face it, will probably be today. Then she'll chop up the rest of my body parts and stitch me into her Frankenstein fuck doll out the back.

I shudder at that revolting memory, too.

I can feel the worms wriggling around deep in my brain and gut and digestive pipeline of despair.

Then I wake up and remember it's real life. My days are dwindling as I drift into terrifying waking hours. My life is now more haunted than a movie.

The maggots and insects wriggle in my every open wound, their disgusting mouths tickling and tearing at me. The endless flies in this oppressive, humid Sydney heat, infesting my flesh.

My owner, Mistress Misery, smears rotten cat food all over my body. The swarm of hungry insect sci-fi mouths burrowed into my flesh. Sucking my blood and life force straight from me.

Like I siphoned the souls from my server of insipid bitches.

Miss Misery is the most sadistic bitch of all.

Out of all the other women stalking Smoke Shadow Kitten, she was the most sinister. I certainly never saw her coming, that's for sure.

Miss Misery never gives us any pain meds. Even when she ripped out all my teeth with a set of rusty fencing pliers in her filthy backyard torture shed. Then inserted some stones in my jawbone instead.

I'm always kept alone but always surrounded by her menagerie of evil-doers. That place where she stitches the corpses of humans together like a fucking doll. She terrifies me more than any masked man.

When she pulled my 'ratty teeth', she just spat whiskey in my face and told me that I should have been kinder to all people. Not just the ones that could help me smash a glass ceiling.

The swarm of tiny, stinking German cockroaches slides over my face, into my ears, into my mouth, and I realize I'm awake and not dreaming again. Up and down my nose they crawl like a little army, tickling my ears, nesting in my brain. I've given up brushing the flies away months ago.

The leeches they throw at me just return if I manage to peel them off, so I don't care anymore. I scratch in my sleep.

The critters and bugs and spiders are dripping in my blood. I fall asleep again. What is real anymore? What is my name anyway? I can't remember.

How long have I been here?

She says, "Happy Halloween!" every damn day, so I have no fucking idea what time means anymore.

So.

I scratch myself again, and retch as the scent of many women's fetid urine overwhelms me.

Misery was the one who was always playing with him in the zombie game. She always came to save him with her strategic and impressive combat moves and skill with weapons.

Now it makes sense. She does have a skill with weapons. It's just that she favours needles and knives, not the automatic guns she used to save Callsign Smoke Shadow Daddy's ass.

I think about his sexy ass, hose glistening piercings, his deep, sultry voice as he jerked himself to climax four times a day.

Now I hear his sexy voice sniffling and crying in Misery's stinky pet corner.

Miss Misery was one of his fans, lurking in his basement. She was the one he wanted.

Little Mousey sneezes from somewhere above me, her hair matted and crawling with lice.

And now we listen to Smoke Kitten stuffed in his dog cage — he still gets most of her attention — on the other side of the room. She got him exactly where she wanted him.

Chained at the ankle to a dog cage. Eating cat food. His balls are sitting in a jar on her bedside table, and his sack is stitched together with God knows what with this bitch.

We, the Disco bitches, are stacked in her creepy Halloween closet like a server farm — or a hen farm — full of depressed, bald hens. We are living in this piss-reeking slum of a madwoman.

Mistress Misery smokes weed and drinks whiskey, tea and rants at us nonstop.

Her insane Crow friends come around any hour of the day or night, just to torment me, poke me with rusty nails or burn me with their cigars. Laugh at me. Pity me.

I can only cry as they spit in my face and pull my hair. spray me with god-knows-who's urine.

They call me a bully, but they're the biggest bullies of all. I'm their villain, and they are mine.

I listen as my god, Smoke Shadow Kitten, or whatever his real name is, whimpers in his sleep. My neck aches, and Maggot wails and sobs, squashed upside down on her head.

Miss Misery shouts at us from her bed.

"This is what mean girls get when the Crows catch wind of you. They found you lurking in some vile spaces. And now you are where you belong, the illustrious STINKY PET STACKS! Aren't you all so lucky! To end up where you wanted to be from the first place? Sleeping with Callsign Smoke Shadow Kitten Ashtray? You're where you belong, with all the other rats and maggots. Now shut the fuck up, and go to nightmare town, bitches. I've got some new product on the move over the next week, and I'll be leaving you to fend for yourselves while I'm gone."

[52]

KITTEN LONELYFACE

IT'S BEEN days since she visited us. I do not know where she's been. The stench of death seeping from the RATTY STACKED CUPBOARD is unbearable. She laid down plastic, so I guess she knew what was coming.

My tummy hurts. I'm so hungry. I need a vape. Her creepy eyes stare at me in my memory.

There have to be at least four women in cages in various states of decomposition. I stare at the sludge of death seeping out from the bottom of the door and spreading in a syrupy pool.

The water container has been empty for a day, and I fear she's leaving us all here.

With the faintest hint of smoke intertwined with the putrid stench of death, my senses are on high alert.

If this house is on fire, I'm toast, literally.

I look across the room. The fat dude with the beard died yesterday, and he doesn't stink like the others. Yet.

But Fluff isn't here, so she must have taken him with her. God only knows what she has planned for that poor fucker.

I sniff the air again, yes. It's smoke.

This is it.

This is the end.

I'm Callsign Smoke Shadow Daddy, goddamn it.

I make women squirt with my microphone and voice, and a smidge of reverb.

THE FUCKING END

Wow.

Congratulations. You made it, my weird little freakish goblin friend.

Now you need to erase this book from your memory, MIB style.

If you made it here, please, turn the page and cut out your gold star.

Remember, don't run with scissors.

WE ARE THE WEIRDOS MISTER

Well, here's your star.

ACKNOWLEDGMENTS

Mr Graves. My everything. Always. I love you.

To my literary coven of clitches. Let's have a circle jerk with our latest books, hit publish, and do it all over again.

And to the ethical, professional voice actors and Dommes out there, this is **not** about you. But we knew that, anyway.

ABOUT THE WEIRDO WORDSMITH

Ivy Graves is a queer gremlin from the land down under. She/they/it is 100% brat with a dirty mind and gutter mouth. But don't let that fool you.

The BDSM lifestyle, cinema, music, fashion, pop culture and art are but a few sources of inspiration. Specifically, the genres of horror, erotica, science fiction, gothic noir, true crime, and the list goes on.

love is love
trans lives matter
don't be a cunt
http://linktr.ee/ivygravesart
https://www.tiktok.com/@ivygravesart

Come and follow me on TIKTOK. I go live regularly and mentor new authors. I talk books, the writing process, and everything to do with books, magic, and the meaning of life. Feel free to get in touch via my email ivygravesauthor@gmail.com if you have any questions. And don't forget to leave a review on all platforms. These small gestures help support indie authors like me.